GOOD WAS THE DAY
The Life of John Fitzgerald Kennedy

Dorothy Davies

GOOD WAS THE DAY
The Life of John Fitzgerald Kennedy

ZADKIEL

PUBLISHING

Good Was The Day

Evensong,
From Cromwell and Other Poems by John Drinkwater.
David Nutt, 1913

Come, let us tell it over,
Each to each by the fireside,
How that earth has been a swift adventure for us,
And the watches of the day as a gay song and a right
song,
And now the traveller has found a bed,
And the sheep crowd under the thorn.

Good was the day and our travelling,
And now there is evensong to sing.

Night, and along the valleys
Watch the eyes of the homesteads.
The dark hills are very still and still are the stars,
Patiently under the ploughlands the wheat moves and the
barley,
The secret hour of love is upon the sky,
And our thought in praise is aflame.

Sing evensong as well we may
For our travel upon this Sabbath day.

Earth, we have known you truly,
Heard your mutable music,
Have been your lovers and felt the savour of you,
And you have quickened in us the blood's fire and the
heart's fire,
We have wooed and striven with you and made you ours
By the strength sprung out of your loins.

Lift the latch on its twisted thong,

And an end be made of our evensong.

From Immortality by John Drinkwater
Olton Pools, Sidgwick and Jackson Ltd.,1917

There in the midst of all these words shall be
Our names, our ghosts, our immortality.

I don't think anyone should write their autobiography
until after they're dead.
Samuel Goldwyn

Dedication

Jack Kennedy would like to dedicate his book first to his wife Jacqueline Bouvier Kennedy, second to all members of his family, past and present and third to all his true friends. They know who they are.

He would like to acknowledge the tremendous feat achieved by Barack Obama, fighting all the odds to become the first African-American President. Jack wishes him well in his term of office and his future life. He also sends his sincere and heartfelt thanks and love to Dorothy for channelling his book.

Dorothy wishes to dedicate this book to the memory of John Fitzgerald Kennedy, 29th May 1917 – 22nd November 1963, in recognition of the service he gave his country and the world.

And to Dorothy Rose Hansen, late of Richland, Washington, USA. We exchanged letters for forty-four years, never meeting but having the unique and wonderful friendship only letter writing can produce, for in the written word is the honesty that builds a true relationship. She is still sadly missed.

Note: This book was started in 2015, during President Barack Obama's second term of office. The work stopped and the book was allowed to mature quietly for two years. This will explain the references to President Obama in the opening chapters.

Preliminary Days

When John Fitzgerald Kennedy began to think about his life story.

I sat for some time, wondering how to convey to people what it meant to be John Fitzgerald Kennedy, 35th President of the United States of America.

I considered the position from all angles, working out my feelings and choosing my words. It seemed to take an age, but finally I began to speak to the channel who would translate those words into the computer.

To be President is a privilege and an honour granted to very few people and whilst it can be said to be the choice of the people, the truth is you have to be someone quite outstanding to make your way through the preliminaries and final stages of what is an extremely arduous period of campaigning. There are times when you wish you did not have to make another speech, to spend time shaking hands, smiling even though your face is aching, discussing or even arguing points of policy with your opponents without losing your temper, wondering if you would ever again live without the glare of spotlights, the ever-present cameras photographing your every expression, capturing with microphones your every word, and then you realise the only thing that is truly yours is your mind. When you accept that your thoughts are inviolate, sacred and very secret, all else becomes bearable. But not until that realisation dawns and sometimes it is a long time coming.

To be President is to have the ultimate in power. In history there have been powerful monarchs who took part in battles, caused the deaths of thousands of people and were responsible for executions at all levels: to them this must have seemed to be the ultimate in power. The President of the United States goes much further than that. For a start the population of the United States is entirely his responsibility. How many millions is that? He has the key which controls the launch of nuclear weapons. How incredible is that? In his hands, literally, is the future of the planet. He has the power to invade another country if he deems it right to do so, to send American troops to their death in the name of liberty. How incredible is that!

This is power on a level, or should that be, at a height few people can appreciate and even fewer actually attain. It is heady, it is an aphrodisiac; it is – beyond words.

To hear the words 'Mr President' for the first time brings a thrill that cannot be replicated by any other act. I know this for I tried everything possible to put that thrill back into my life, without success. I was concerned that it would become commonplace and I didn't want that. I didn't want to get to the point when I would wake in the morning and think 'it's just another day.' I believe the office of President is of such magnitude it is impossible to describe unless you have lived it.

To walk through the White House, to sit at the presidential desk, to know telephones link you to the other incredibly powerful people in this world and all you have to do is to pick up the receiver and speak with them, gives you a sense of unbelievable supremacy. I realise I am labouring the point but how else can I get the reader to understand just how it felt to hold that position? Even when the popularity ratings went down, as they always do after a successful election, it doesn't matter because whoever is elected has the power for at least four years, provided death or illness or insanity does not intervene. Any or all of them could happen... the job is that pressurised! If at the end of four years you have to surrender the White House to someone else, that doesn't matter, either. You will always be remembered as a President of the United States.

What it means in practice is: that person can never go back to what they once thought of as 'normal' life. Everything they do is governed by the fact of once being President. Wherever they go, whatever sport they take up, they are an ex-President, reported, photographed, consulted, invited, guarded, protected and wealthy.

Unless, of course, they were 'fortunate' enough to be assassinated and so go out with all the glory that an assassination bestows.

I mused on the question, was I sad when it ended so abruptly?

In truth I had to say 'No'. There was much I wanted to do which had to be left to someone else to carry on, but no, I was not sad when it was over - for one very big reason.

On the 23rd June 2010 I made a momentous decision. I decided to tell the world why I was not sad that my life ended on that November day in Dallas. Up to and including 22nd June 2010 I had held firm to my decision not to speak of it. In fact, my channel had been working on another book; that author kindly stepped aside to allow me to dictate the words so a record could be made of the decision.

The fact was, if I had planned my own assassination, if I had paid the assassin, it could not have been better timing for the Kennedy family, or for the United States. Only now, as the 50th anniversary of my assassination draws near, the secret that had bothered me; almost haunted me I might say, for fifty years, can be revealed so that I can at last find a degree of peace.

Contemplative Days

When time was spent working out how to tell the story of
John Fitzgerald Kennedy

I looked at the blank screen, at my channel patiently waiting and all but panicked. Where did I start, truthfully? With the Kennedy clan which made us all what we were? When I first realised I was a man who adored women? What was it the readers would really like to know about me? The prologue was over; the first thoughts were in place. Now came the really hard part.

I left my channel's office, returned to my home and began to pace, glancing at the walls where family photos were displayed to remind me of what the Kennedys once were, a powerful, influential and very rich family, tainted in some areas, venerated in others. I thought of those who praised the family and me, then of those who hated the family and me; idly wondering who, out of all those who carried hate, felt the emotion fiercely enough to arrange my death. Was Oswald the one who fired the killing shot? Films I have seen since my death say no. Conspiracy theories abounded but they always do when someone high profile is killed. In this case, though, it seems they were very likely right. To my mind, the killer has not been found. As with all good paid assassins, and I am one hundred per cent sure the gunman was a professional, he got clean away and someone else took the rap. Someone else died; someone who was probably innocent of killing me. But who can prove anything? That's another matter entirely. Can't prove a thing from this side of the divide, I thought. What I can do, though, is write about the events that led up to that single shot moment. The one that killed me.

Hmm, single shot moment. Nearly a title for a thriller there, if I had been so inclined. No, I had enough to do putting my life story together and sorting out some of the rubbish that has appeared in print over the last fifty years. So much has been written about me, some of it true, some false, some halfway between the two and some so outrageous I wonder where the writers got it from, asking myself what sort of distorted imagination came up with the 'facts' presented in written form for people to read. There is a problem with that, when people see something in print, they tend to believe it even if it is so outrageous and stupid it can't possibly be true. Ah, they would say, it could be true...

How much of what has been written about the Kennedys, how much of what continues to be written about Jack Kennedy and the family came from minds which are free of bias? How many people continue, even after all this time, to be jealous of what the Kennedys achieved? And as for my errors, my misjudgements... no man is perfect, whether he be the President of the United States or a street cleaner. Everyone comes with guilts, sins, imperfections, obsessions, fears, hates, loves and, most of all, that driving ambition which pushes people on even when the odds are stacked against them. Was the jealousy because of their own inadequacies, the realisation that they did not have the drive, the determination, to push ahead and change their lives and those of their fellow citizens? Who knows? But it was there, and it was real.

Back to my life story. I lived a very full, varied and complicated life. I need to try and explain it from my perspective, rather than from letters, conversations, film clips and all the other sources a biographer has. It has to be feelings; it has to be different, why else would anyone want to read it?

I have to admit to my channel that this preamble is going on somewhat and that's because I have still to pin down the point at which I wish to start this story.

The trouble is - I'm not sure how much the reader will want to know, or more importantly, how much I'm able to tell them. In truth, I know they will want to know it all and some things can't be revealed, even now. It is one thing for an author to say, "I'm going to be honest with you" and quite another to be as openly honest as the reader would hope for. Of necessity there are things that each author would not be able to speak of, whether that be political, religious, or quite simply being incapable of speaking of it. That is only human. So, where to begin?

At the start, where else?

Oh yes, at the start, but before then, I realise I still have things I want to say.

The simple fact is, I need to say first, if you fight your way through to becoming a Senator and go ever onward and upward, if you are fortunate enough to be chosen by your compatriots and your countrymen to be their president, even if it is not by a huge majority of the voters, you end up with the ultimate power of ruling the world.

No matter what the world's opinion is of any president who held office, people had to admit this: they were all, in their own way, outstanding men. Even those who stepped from the vice presidency to the presidential office were outstanding men. They had to be to gain the vice presidency nomination in the first place. Individual opinion on any of these people is varied, of course, remembering that no two people see the third person in the same light anyway. It may be considered that some of them were ineffectual and others an unmitigated disaster, but the world remembered them. People may not remember the person who served in the shop today but presidents, yes, the world remembers them.

Presidents have had books written about them, books full of their foolish comments, they may have been the butt of many jokes, but there is that one abiding fact – the world remembers them. And presidents wrote their own books; I did that, ensuring lasting fame of some kind at least.

I am very aware I am viewed on either side of the Atlantic in a different way. I know that some of my people did not hold me in high regard, but that was to be expected. No one could be expected to be liked by everyone; they had to come to terms with their policies not being accepted by the country as a whole. The opposing party would always find holes and flaws and difficulties in everything that was proposed or passed. In the UK, where this book will be published, I know that some held me in high regard which made a big difference to the way I felt. I want to say that was not the reason I happen to have an English channel for this book, it just happens that the channel who is prepared to write the book for me is English, but it suits me well that she is.

I was happy with the way I was – and to some degree still am - regarded in the UK. I have to hope the book will cast some further light on me, Jack Kennedy, ex-President of the United States and perhaps the regard of my fellow countrymen will rise a little because of it - if they care to read it. That is, of course, if the book sells in the United States. I can but hope - on both counts.

Then I ask myself why it matters so much. I cannot influence anything that goes on in the United States or in England - or should I say Great Britain? I thought it might be part of my ego which has remained intact even after all these years, blaming that for the fact I still place a degree of importance in the way people perceive me. I still don't know.

But there is a need and for this reason and for my need to settle my mind on the secret I carry, the book has to be written. The difficulty remains that I am not sure how much I can talk about, how much should be left out, what should be fully revealed, what would satisfy the reader.

15

During my time in office, many momentous things happened. During my life many momentous things happened. One of the major happenings was my marriage. I adored my wife (I still do) and kept her at the centre of my world at all times. Without her I believe my presidency would have been a good deal more difficult than it actually was. But there were others, oh, how many others! It is extremely difficult for a man, a virile man, to refuse that which is offered to him over and over again. Beautiful women, intelligent women, some with ambitions, some with aspirations they could not quite formulate, some who just thought that getting close to the source of power would be enough to set them on a new life path and some who simply loved me. I have to say, in truth, that those who simply loved me were the ones I loved the most. With the others I was ever aware they had their own agenda for being in the relationship. That was something I had to remember at all times when I was with them.

What most of the women did not understand was that holding the ultimate power on this earth did not mean I was entirely my own person. I could not drop everything if they asked me; I could not get in a car and drive to wherever they happened to be when they wanted me to. I was ever surrounded by secret servicemen and I was ever regulated by the diary, which was unrelenting and unforgiving. There were priorities, of course. The first was the United States of America which came before everything. Then there was consideration for the family, the children who needed to see their father from time to time. They were, after all, a part of me and I could not just put them to one side. After that came the demands of the office itself, the diplomatic meetings, the cocktail parties; the speeches on the lawn, the wandering around the Rose Garden with this leader or that; making small talk, often through a translator. Each twenty-four hours was tightly regulated by other people. Within that stricture, I needed to make time for women. A lot of them.

It wasn't easy.

Nor is attempting to write my book. My channel demands much of me, not facts, but feelings. They are a good deal more difficult to describe, to relive, to actually put into words. But I have to try because if I don't, my one chance to find peace of mind will be lost, perhaps forever.

Early Days

The making of John Fitzgerald Kennedy

Right. The contemplating is done, I believe.

I know there are many books on my life, many extensive articles on my life, too. That is leaving aside the conspiracy theory, which has also been written about at great length. So, I thought, if anyone wants the details of my early life, my schooling, my family, my whole background, they can go and find any of the books on my life in any bookshop or library in their area. If I was to repeat all of that, this book would be tremendously thick and would give the reader nothing which they could not have found somewhere else.

I know that what I really have to talk about is not in those books, it is what is in my head and heart – that which runs deep in me. I rationalised, in discussions with my channel, that anyone who writes a biography has to make a guess at how their subject felt about certain things. They could only do this by talking to others, or in the case of people long dead, by speculation. It is because of this limitation that 99% of biographies are flawed. In truth, many autobiographies are also flawed, because the authors, for their own reasons, distorted or even hid some facts that would be revealing, too revealing perhaps, to the reader.

The authors who are no longer 'living' do not have that problem. If they decide to tell the truth about something, they can do it, even if there are people still alive who knew them. As far as this book is concerned, it is very likely that those people will protest and say 'of course it was not like that. Of course Jack did not do...' whatever it was that had been written. The fact is; when spirit authors come to speak on the subject of their lives, they only speak the truth. There is no point in doing anything else. I need to say that before anyone insists this is not me, not my words. It is. Accept it.

It is time to embark on the story of the life of John Fitzgerald Kennedy as seen by John Fitzgerald Kennedy, utilising modern technology to bring my words to the reader via the most ancient of communications – that from one side of the divide to the other, my words to my channel via the link we have formed, one of mutual respect, trust and affection.

I thought; if I were to find one word to describe my life it would be 'competition'. The Kennedys were a large family and, within that group, if we wanted to make a mark on the world, even a world as small as the family home, we were in competition with the others. Joe Kennedy was a man we all strove to emulate for he seemed to have a certain power and ability which took him into many different places with many different people and which ultimately gave us all a very good living.

As a man, though, he seemed remote, ever concerned with politics and business, with making his mark on his world in his own way. What dealings he had, what people he dealt with, he alone knew most of the time. Much has been written about my father but that did not go to the very heart of the man and his empire, some of which would never be known – and it is better left that way, too. Perhaps because of that the family as a whole revered him.

It has not escaped my attention that I begin my life story with my father. It is a measure of his influence on us all that I do so. Somehow it does not seem right to do anything else.

That in turn leads to my mother.

My mother appeared to adore my father and consequently to turn a blind eye to much that he did, rather than disrupt their way of life. What women he had, what dealings he had with less than salubrious people, she overlooked. She was a dedicated hostess and political wife, but not a natural mother. It was as if she lived in a self-contained, enclosed world. She was not a comforting, loving mother, the kind you could go to for hugs and love. Not as far as I was concerned, anyway. Whether my brothers and sisters felt differently, I do not know. It wasn't something you asked. You accepted.

It was clear to us Kennedy boys that no matter how well Bobby or Teddy or I did in life, we did not equal - and would not equal - the firstborn, Joe. The family ambitions rested on him, he was the one destined for Great Things in the world. The rest of us were left to make our own way in life. The poor mentally disabled sister, well, no one spoke of her, she was hidden away at home, as if she was an embarrassment. Joe Kennedy only wanted the All-American family to be shown to everyone who mattered.

As a family we moved often, each time to a better place so that people could see and appreciate the Kennedys going up in the world. Every one of us had aspirations, dreams and desires which we did not speak to each other about at the time. Only later, when we were adults, did we discuss that which we planned to do - and be.

I also realised, very early on, that girls were attracted to me. I would look in the mirror and see a reasonable face looking back. To me it was nothing extraordinary, as in, I was not sure I could be classed as handsome or even good-looking and was extremely surprised, as well as pleased, to find that I was viewed this way. In hindsight I date this as the beginning of the development of the massive JFK ego. If anyone had asked how big that ego was, I would have been forced to say that this planet was not big enough to contain it... It would have been easy to say, oh, it was about the size of the White House, but in truth it was much, much bigger than that. My beloved Jackie knows this and is standing by to make sure it doesn't intrude too much on my book... but I ask you, a book about myself, my life, my presidency, my women... surely it has to be the biggest ego trip of all, does it not?

Onward! If someone wishes to be noticed, if they wish to stand out from the crowd, they have to be different. They have to develop a style, a charisma or an intellect of the kind which makes others admire them, or they have to be blessed with startling good looks and/or an outstanding talent for acting, music, writing, or singing. If anyone thinks of the singers and actors who have been outstanding during their lives, they realise one thing; they were different. The same thing applies to musicians and writers.

When people are young, it is not easy to understand this. Until someone becomes an adult and sometimes even when they are an adult, they are subject to peer pressure and have a bad habit of doing 'follow my leader' with the strongest or best-looking person in the group. For some reason man is still very tribal in his thinking: members of a group tend to dress the same, wear their hair the same, go to the same places, use the same slang, all of which is designed to indicate to the outside world that these individuals are one.

I confess to the pages of my book that I did not understand this when I eventually went to boarding school, the one which my brother Joe already attended. Joe had his own group of friends and followers, his own clique and I was just the 'younger Kennedy brother'. But in my head I had never been just 'the younger brother' and was determined I would not be so in school, either. There are records of the many escapades in which I indulged at that time, all of it designed to draw attention to Jack Kennedy as a person, not as a 'younger brother.' I knew that I would one day make a mark on the world, not for escapades of a foolish nature, but for doing something for the people of the USA. I told no one of this, it would have brought derision onto my head and that was one thing I could not have tolerated.

Secrets, everyone has them.

School Days
Learning to live with others and tolerate them

Boarding school came as a great shock. No home comforts, shared everything, communal bathing, eating, sleeping, games, lessons, study times, all this created a desperate need for privacy and calm, if for no other reason than to think. It was a completely alien way of life for me as a young boy, it meant putting on a face that the school and the other boys would recognise as acceptance of the status quo whilst inside there was a desperate longing to return home even if that home was not the oasis of comfort and love I would have wished. Most, if not all, of this was not realised at the time, it has only become clear during adult life, when I can look back and understand the futile longings often obsessing me at that time.

So that small boy found himself an even smaller fish in a very big pond indeed. I had two choices: I could either retire into myself, become a recluse, a swot in effect, or I could become an extrovert, gather some friends around me and make an impression on the others, everyone from the next age-group upwards to the staff at the school. It took me two or three days to assess the situation before I decided to go for the extrovert option. I was very glad I took that course; it gave me a good grounding for my future life, especially in the Marines. It also helped when I became a congressman. But all that was in the far distant future and not thought about at that time. The priority was to survive, to be top rather than underdog, to be accepted socially and academically and in doing so to ensure that the world -- for which read the school -- realised that John F. Kennedy was a person in his own right. Even at that young age, it was extremely important to me to do that.

The one thing I found I could do was make friends easily. Whether or not they were lasting friendships did not matter at the time; all that concerned me was having a gang to hang out with, to make school that much better, to show the world that I too had friends. My brother could do as he wished. I wanted to live my own life. Later I realised that this was in fact rather foolish, as family are sometimes better friends than friends. I thought this, whilst knowing I had some extremely good, loyal friends, people I thought a great deal of, but the Kennedys always came first. Maybe it was something we grew up with, maybe it was the result of the way we grew up; maybe it was the pressures of the time. I didn't really know. Most likely it was a combination of all of that.

The foolish thing was that even whilst I maintained the stance of allowing my brother to do as he wished, and I lived my own life, us brothers were very strongly involved with one another. It was there the competition was the fiercest, Joe against me, me against Joe, to the point of bloodshed at times, fights and arguments with family that did not really sit well with me, but the competitive element between us was so strong that I took part in it willingly. There were minor skirmishes with Bobby and Teddy and none at all with my sisters. I venerated them as females. Later I became aware that my father sometimes provoked these fights by setting one against the other in an effort to keep the competitive element going. He must have reasoned his boys had to be strong if we were to survive in the USA. That is, if we were to survive as a family with money, status and most of all, power. My father did not seem to mind from where he gained power and had friends which it might have been better if he had not cultivated. Despite this, the family venerated him. His power seemed endless. His word was law.

And you see I am back talking about my father again.

As a family striving for fame and fortune, the Kennedys had one major drawback. We were Irish Catholics. This was not a problem at school; the services were interdenominational for a start. In fact it was something that did not bother me for a long time. It was there, as much as family history is always there, colouring everything anyone does, thinks and feels. As a child the fact we were an Irish Catholic family in a Protestant American society did not appear to create a difficulty, but in later years, when the prejudice became obvious, I fully appreciated the tremendous feat my father had managed to carry off. He had conquered the Irish Catholic background to become ambassador to London, to accumulate wealth beyond most people's dreams, he bought large homes in good neighbourhoods without antagonising the neighbours, he ran for high office and achieved it and never once let the Irish Catholic dog bite at his heels. In a Protestant world, to be openly Catholic and seeking office were two things that did not go together very well. But my father had achieved it. In many ways he was a man to be admired.

Home, when I was allowed to return there, was ever a place of energy, of flux, of instability in some ways, when it should have been an oasis of comfort and security in a child's world. Most people have a room of their own where they can keep their childhood possessions, their clothes and their memories. Most people have a memory of their childhood home, a place they could walk with their eyes closed, knowing every creaking floorboard, every squeaking door, every quirk of the building. I could not do that. We never stayed anywhere overly long; my father was ever moving us on to a bigger and better house with more ground in a better environment and neighbourhood. I never knew which room was mine, I would go away to boarding school and come home and ask which room I was to use. I would have to ask where my books, my possessions, my left-at-home clothes were and usually found them put away in a closet. I would rescue them for the duration of my stay. There was no sense of being rooted, of being secure, of being wrapped around with the comfort of a known and comfortable home. I could not have said how I knew that was not right but in talking with others, visiting friends, seeing that they had their own room with posters on the wall and photographs, mementos of all kinds, sport and things like that, I knew my home was not the same and it bothered me. My memory is of envying them their own room, a vague restless envy that had no real roots in something positive. It was something missing from my life and it was something I aspired to have for myself and knew that when I did I would call it my own.

It is not easy for me as an adult to look back and put myself in the shoes and in the place of that much younger being, but I recall lacking in confidence until I built a group around myself at school, of being in awe of teachers for a while until I realised they were just people doing a job, some of them excellently, some of them adequately, some of them badly and then they lost their mystique for me. I remember struggling with lessons until something seemed to click and then it all flowed, made sense, whether they were talking maths or literature or science or any of the wider subjects. It was as if the lessons had to fight their way in and then, once there, they rooted and sprouted and I knew what it was all about. I excelled at all lessons once this happened. For the first time I was aware that others envied me and that was a good feeling. It helped to build even more confidence.

I remember: reading aloud in class and thinking that I liked the fact all those people were listening to me. There was a sense of power even in that, for when I read, no one shifted or scraped their chair or coughed or did anything to distract me or show their lack of interest.

I remember: fighting and recall, even after all this time, the taste of blood but much, much more than that, the taste of fear – the fear of losing. In my mind, losing was not to be tolerated. I won every fight and later, every argument in debate - in class or out. Reasoned logic overcame emotional outbursts, knowing the facts better than your opponent worked every time. It did later in my life, too, but at that time I had no plans to go into politics, it was a 'maybe' ambition. But at the time, oh at the time it was a mantra for me:

Be in control.

Be the one everyone listens to.

Be the one who wins fights fair and square against a worthy opponent.

Be the winner.

Be the victor.

Wear the laurel wreath, accept the cup; proudly wear the medal.

A boy's dreams.

A man's dreams.

Who can say what a boy dreams when he is young and impressionable and open to all sorts of influences and thoughts?

And who can say how much family impresses itself upon you in the early years, leaving a residue which accompanies you into the later years?

I find it impossible to say just how much of an influence my family had but it was considerable. How much was them, how much was school, teachers and pupils, how much was my own personality and drive?

The Roman Catholic faith which was the backbone of the family became my backbone too as time went on. Without that, I might have been left floundering in a world that was not friendly at the best of times and I was to experience many bad times as well as 'best of times'.

Being a Kennedy meant we all strove to be better than anyone else, we had the very best that our father could provide, good schools, homes in 'good' locations, places to go for holidays and always, always what I thought of as the clan supporting and caring and loving and arguing and oft times fighting - for we were all individuals in our own way. Some family members had aspirations beyond the clan: I knew I did. At times it was not enough to be just a Kennedy. I wanted more than that; I wanted to climb the social ladder, to mix with those who had the power as well as the money to change people's lives. It was something I really wanted to do; I really wanted that power and that money. For the longest time I could not see how to get it, it nagged at me, it worried me, for I knew I would not be content until I achieved it. It was back to that taste of fear, fear of losing. That was not something I could contemplate.

I knew, and admit, that at that time my prayers were more on the basis of; 'please give me the strength to achieve that which I desire so much', rather than 'give me the strength to be a loving son and brother and member of my family.' I also confess I never ever told the priest this! There were some things, some driving ambitions, which I did not feel I could confess even to a priest. They went too deep.

But without those burning ambitions, life would have washed over me and possibly carried me away in its currents. With everything geared to Joe Jnr. being the heir apparent to the Kennedy empire, everyone else was relegated to the lower levels. I knew this and knew I had to fight, in every way possible, to break through and be my own person, to live my life my way.

Later in my life, school, no matter where it was or what it was, became relatively easy for me. As I said, as soon as I realised the logic behind the teaching, the learning, the examinations, the good results and all came easy. It did not come easy to my friends who looked at me with envy and even awe at times, which gave me secret pleasure. It was back to that 'being the centre of attention' syndrome again. That was something only maturity has shown me, at the time it was just something I felt, absorbed and added to my driving ambition.

Days of Chronic Ill health

The bigger lessons, learning to cope with pain

Throughout all this I had a major problem that would haunt my entire life. To put it mildly, I did not suffer the best of health. In fact I seemed to spend an inordinate amount of time in hospital, which disrupted my schooling – and my plans. I had a problem with my appendix, something over which I had no control but the other problems which plagued me, my back, my stomach, these I looked upon as a weakness of my body and despised it. Weakness was not to be tolerated under any circumstances; ill-health had no part to play in my future plans. To dream of being of service to your country was one thing when you were fit and well and capable of taking on just about anything, but being ill, suffering chronic pain from a back condition, that put a whole new perspective on driving ambition. Resentment at being forced to rest did not make me a good patient. But then, what boy of that age makes a good patient anyway? Lying in a hospital bed was not the best way to pass the days when there was so much to do. It was made worse by my aversion to the seemingly never-ending tests for this, that, for the other and then they would come back and start all over again. The family visited when they could, but had busy lives and time passed when I would see no-one I loved. It did not make hospital any easier to endure.

What it did was give me time to contemplate where I wanted to go and what I wanted to do. It was during these times I decided I would go into one of the forces when I was old enough. It seemed like a good idea, as most things do, when viewed long distance. The thought of exchanging a sterile hospital environment for the rough and tumble of a group of people who were there for one thing and one thing only, to serve their country, seemed like a good trade. That too was something I kept strictly to myself and I was merely apathetically polite to those who visited from time to time.

When I was 'released' from hospital, and that's how it felt to me, I had an invitation to go to London. I was offered the opportunity of studying at the London School of Economics. For someone who had wanted to travel but had not been given the chance, this was a great adventure.

The journey from the USA to England was an adventure in itself. I found pleasure in listening to the different voices, people who spoke without what seemed like a harsh accent. I became used to the different money and shops, the general climate that was England but I did not enjoy my studies at the LSE. For some reason I was incapable of settling to the work. In truth, I found many opportunities to avoid the lectures, because there was always something more interesting to do, that 'something' I freely admit, centred around nubile young women.

Strange though it may seem, even that palled after a while, so I returned to the USA where I enrolled in Princeton University. It had long been an ambition to go there so I went, with great hopes of settling into a new period of study and the possibility of choosing my future career.

It seemed, though, that life was determined to stop me doing this as almost immediately I became ill and was hospitalised yet again. This time it was serious, the doctors suspected leukaemia and poked and prodded and took blood and tested and came back and poked and prodded some more. I didn't think they really knew what was wrong with me once leukaemia was ruled out. The first verdict terrified me; I had visions of the slow decline that the illness would bring, of never fulfilling my dream and, in truth, of not having had my fill of women. I knew if I had leukaemia, I would leave this life full of regrets. That, more than anything, coloured the way I saw the rest of my days. Every opportunity that was given to me, I took. Any woman who offered herself, I took. Any opportunity to further myself or to add to my dream, I took. I was determined that when I died, and I did not expect to live very long, I had no regrets.

Obviously, at this point of my life I was not a very fit person. I had suffered several periods of hospitalisation, endless tests and been seen by goodness knows how many consultants, none of whom appeared to know what was wrong with me. I felt I needed some kind of overhaul, a new physical regime, something to test my strength and increase it. I reasoned that I could not be outstanding if I was ill. Once the doctors agreed to let me go, I decided to work as a ranch hand where I could spend a good deal of time riding and getting involved in physical work in the fresh air. In my opinion, this did me more good than any tonic. At the back of this decision was my intense aversion to constantly ending up in a hospital bed. I felt I could not tolerate the intrusive doctors with their tests, blood samples, thermometers and everything else they seemed to drag around with them. It was almost as if they carried them all as a badge of office, rather than something they needed.

I would say to them, 'why don't you know what's wrong with me?'

And they would say, 'Well, we do, but we need to test you for this and that...'

I would respond by saying, 'that's not the answer I was looking for. My question was, why do you not know what's wrong with me? After all, you're the ones who've been through medical school, not I.' But they would waffle on, using medical terms which the layman could not understand, which was designed to make them seem all-powerful, all knowing, almost invincible. I detected a certain lack of knowledge which they tried to hide behind this medical talk. The truth was they really did not know what was wrong with me, I thought. Whatever I was suffering from, it was not a common condition. I just had to hope that one day somebody would be able to diagnose it properly and then be able to treat it.

The gamble paid off. Working on the ranch I became fitter, stronger, revelling in the freedom of being able to ride, to work without someone watching my every move. I slept well, ate well and came back to the family a man on a mission: to attain my goals, my dreams.

The True Harvard Man

*More development for the person who would become
President John Fitzgerald Kennedy*

With Princeton nothing more than a vague unhappy
memory, a lost opportunity, I enrolled in Harvard. I
needed a degree, I needed to finish my education, here
was a chance and I took it, as I had taken so many
others.

My first impression was of the overwhelming size
of the campus. I felt as if I would never find my way
around, the buildings were huge, the amount of students
quite phenomenal, the awe-inspiring church made an
immediate impression on me. I was a small fish in a
huge pond this time, a pond created many years before I
came into this life. That in itself was awesome to me.
There was a tremendous sense of history, it being the
oldest university in the United States and that history
seemed to weigh heavily on the buildings and everything
associated with it. At some point the colour crimson had
been adopted as the University colour. It was
everywhere. I became aware that I was looking for it all
the time and finding it. It added to the mystique of the
place and yet it almost felt as if I had come home.

All too soon the sense of awe vanished and
everything became commonplace. In some ways I
thought that was a shame, in other ways I was grateful
because it meant I was settling down. Harvard was good
for me, despite the fact I was once again following in my
brother's footsteps. There I seemed to be able to make
my mark as Jack Kennedy, rather than Joe Kennedy's
younger brother. It made all the difference to the way I
felt and I knew that my ambition to be different, to be
some kind of leader, was one step nearer than it had
been. It was almost as if Harvard lent itself to ambition,
to ambitious young men, to the facility to make dreams
become reality. In reality, though, the only thing which

made dreams come true was commitment, determination and drive.

Nothing happened unless you made it happen.

To make it happen you have to set your heart and mind to it and not allow yourself to be sidetracked.

That was my philosophy, my motto, my mantra and I never ever let go of it. I walked and talked the dream and because of that, in the end it happened - but only after a good deal of hard work on my part. Work such as I could never have envisaged at that time. I wondered if I had been able to see into the future, to gauge what a toll the work would take of my health, my life, my family, whether I would have gone ahead with it. Sometimes, I mused, it is best that we don't know what lies ahead for surely we would turn back, change direction, avoid the hardships, but would we be better people for doing that, or worse?

In this new world, this new environment, where I found myself respected for what I was, not for who I was, I began to develop into the man I was to become. In my social life I became very close to a lot of women but I had, by then, learned how to shut doors. There were things I simply did not speak of, subjects that were on the 'forbidden list', as it were. One thing I did not discuss with outsiders was family, one thing I did not discuss with family were the women I met. In between those two was the totally secret territory that was - and - is the mind and ambitions and dreams of John Fitzgerald Kennedy.

I stopped for a moment and looked at the words my channel has put onto the screen. I wondered at the freedom I felt to talk openly about my ambitions and dreams at that time but then realised that part of the freedom is because there is no one to influence those ambitions and dreams any more, or indeed anything else I planned to do. What I did, what I said, was entirely in my hands and no one can accuse me of anything should I leave this out or talk on that instead, for I remain beyond the reproach of the reader. It is for me to choose how much to tell the reader of my life at that time. My problem is, so much happened to me after that time it was hard for me to remember what the rather gauche, often self-conscious young man was actually feeling.

That in itself will be a surprise to many, I mused, for I knew I gave the appearance of someone who knew exactly what they wanted, where they were going and had their life plan securely in place at all times. The truth is; I did not. There will be those who will say I did not come over as gauche, that the good manners which were literally inbred were always evident. Maybe they were; that did not take into account how I felt. No one knew of all my hopes, ambitions and dreams, all of which contributed to the making of John Fitzgerald Kennedy.

Incidentally, I want to say I did – and still do – like my name. It seems to have a classy ring to it. I don't mind being called Jack, it is after all a good solid old name, but writing or seeing my full name always, always gave –and continues to give me - a tiny twinge of pleasure. Nonsense, of course, but there it is. You want JFK? You get JFK, plain and unvarnished, as I told my channel. Well, almost. She does. I am not sure the reader will...

Family Ties

The role of the Kennedy family in the making of John Fitzgerald Kennedy

During the period of entering this world as a helpless child, through learning to walk and talk, through learning to read and write, through learning what is and is not right, through losing baby teeth and growing adult ones, through watching limbs seemingly grow by the day, through the awkward teenage years when you're not entirely sure what your voice or your body is going to do next and coping with the rush of hormones which send the mood flying in all directions, to the time when I became a Marine, I had the support, the loving atmosphere and the loyalty of the Kennedys. Few people can say that their family is as tight knit as ours. And so each tragedy that we suffered, and we did, diminished all of us because of it. When you are young, you are firmly of the opinion that your parents, your brothers and sisters and your extended family will last forever. Death is an abstract word, it means nothing until a pet dies and you realise what it really means, the going away and never coming back. (Never coming back in a physical sense, that is, for I do not believe anyone will have any doubt that I am most certainly back now, in spirit form, bringing my hard-working English channel a hint of my aftershave and a sense of my powerful presence, as she describes it. I have to say it is the strangest experience to hear my American accent translated into very precise English without an accent and to watch the words appear on screen as if by magic. That is leaving aside the fact I am male and my words are being translated into the computer by a female. Could anything be stranger than that?)

I realise I have created quite a diversion here and realise too I need to go back to what I was saying; the Kennedy clan was everything. We all leaned on each other, even as we argued and fought and fell out regularly, we were still one. My mother made sure of that. My father was the driving influence for all of us, but my mother was the bond. Her strength kept the Kennedys together. She turned a blind eye to things that would have otherwise bothered her, for example, anything Father might be getting up to she would not have cared to know about, visitors who may not have been exactly who they said they were, for in the end it all came down to one thing: survival of the family.

Survival, the ever-present need to improve ourselves; to have a bigger and better home in a bigger and better neighbourhood, was all part of her need. My father had to have the right background to be the person he was, ambassador, Senator and all the other roles he held during my life and he relied on his wife to provide it for him. She was the perfect hostess, the perfect companion, the perfect wife. I knew I had to have a wife like that.

'I did, didn't I?' I asked. Then I thought, that is so bad; it looks very much like 'aren't I a clever boy?' And no, I'm not.

I know I made more mistakes in my life than many other people do or have done, which is in part why I am even now trying to put down the words that will clear my conscience and put things right. As far as the rest of the Kennedy family is concerned, it is not my job to attempt to explain away my father's activities, whatever they were, what my mother endured, tolerated, or enjoyed or what my brothers and sisters did. For anyone looking to this book for the answer to the whole sorry mess of Chappaquiddick, for example, forget it. It is not for me to say. I thought, 'If my brother wishes to speak on it, then he knows where the channel lives and knows too that she will accept him in her life.'

Opting out? I asked myself and gave the answer, 'I don't think so. This is the life of John Fitzgerald Kennedy, not Joe, Rose, Bobby, Teddy, or anyone else. Ever the egocentric, this is my book and this is how it will stay.'

I decided to close this particular section of my book with the words that were used in the Yearbook of Choate School. It is an oddity that such a small thing should please me so much and yet it did. The comment in the 1935 yearbook about JF Kennedy is 'Most Likely To Succeed.'

I did that too, didn't I?

I defy anyone to deny the truth of that statement.

Pre-War Days
The political awakening of John Fitzgerald Kennedy

Diversions were all very well, I thought, provided I remember to go back to the point where I diverted and pick it up again. So I have to do this now...

Harvard College.

Its very name speaks history to any aspiring American. For me it was a natural progression from Choate, one I welcomed. It was about as close as Americans get to history in their country and they are mighty proud of it. When I walked into the grounds on my first day, I felt a sense of history in everything I looked at, everything I touched, everything I heard. Familiarity very soon took that away, that which was extraordinary for a time became ordinary. That, of course, is the natural way of life. I did, however, recall vividly that first day and a great sense of history. I could not say how much it coloured my future life there, I was not overly aware that it did, but for all that the memory remains a fond one, which was why I mention it at this time.

There was much to do, new timetables to remember, new routes to learn to get from this place to that, classrooms, to discover, tutors to remember and, most of all, new friends to make, for me one of the most exciting things about going there.

Although not hundred percent fit (I never was) I tried to get into the football, the golf and swimming, because it is always a Good Thing to be part of a team in a place like Harvard. You need a niche, you need a place; you need a definition. I managed to get a place in the swimming team. It was enough for me and actually helped my health quite a bit. I was never a brilliant swimmer; I never would excel in any kind of sport, but I pulled my weight as part of the team. It was all that mattered to me. How strange, I thought, that I should have been chosen for the swimming team, for that particular activity was to play a major part in my life in the Marines. Had it not been for my extensive training, the outcome of PT109 might have been very different. I paused for a moment, wondering whether in fact it had been planned, then decided that indeed it had.

But I need to go back to Harvard. That immense institution, in every respect, physically and to some degree emotionally, with its incredible reputation, was an extremely important part of my life, not just my education. To be a Harvard man meant a great deal in the business world, it added a certain lustre to one's business acumen and opened doors that would have otherwise remain closed. I was not totally aware of this when I first joined the University as a freshman, but it was something I learned to appreciate in later life. The decisions I took in my young days reflected well in my more adult life and so I was grateful I had the Harvard experience to help me when I set out on my chosen career.

Once the sense of history had gone away and left in its place the familiarity of yet another school, as it were, I settled down to get on with the work of earning my degree. I took part in and had a lot of political discussions, people being very well aware of my father's reputation and that of my brother Joe who preceded me through the same college. We were two years apart in both age and experience. I had a lot of making up to do.

In a family like ours, politics were discussed as freely as the weather. I grew up breathing in the atmosphere all the political parties, all shades of opinion, combined with the sure and certain knowledge that I was a Roman Catholic, where so many others were Protestant. Within the family there were divisions, strongly held opinions, but as far as the outside world was concerned we showed a united front. I believe that this was the beginning of the trend of compartmentalising my life. I learned to show one face to the public, tutors and fellow students, another to priests and attendees at church, yet another to visitors to the house and anyone else that came into my life for whatever reason and then I had a private face which the family saw. To them I was just Jack, important, but not as important as Joe, he being the oldest son, something which perpetually annoyed me. You can take it from that I was developing an ego which was busy growing and which helped to give me the foundation of self-confidence that I sought.

There is no room in a large family for a shy and retiring wallflower. Each of us strove to be an individual, to make ourselves different from the others, to make our mark on the world. It mattered little whether that world was the family home, the neighbourhood, or the United States. Actually, I believe we were all destined to make a mark on the history of the United States in one way or another. I make no claim to being psychic, to having any ability whatsoever to foresee, but I did know that my family was extremely influential in many quarters, starting with my father and ending with my brother Teddy. Good publicity, bad publicity, scandals, rumours and innuendos, good deeds and bad, good connections and bad, all went to make what was undoubtedly a very famous family. To be a Kennedy was sufficient to open many doors in many places and I freely admit I unashamedly used the family influence to get what I wanted when I wanted it. I ask, would you not have done the same? Anyone who has that kind of influence, that kind of powerful family at the back of them, would be foolish not to make the utmost use of it.

I would also say that much of what I did, achieved and obtained in my short lifetime was due to my own efforts. Even though I used the family connections, it was my drive and personal ambition which took me from the lowest ranks of the political scene to the very highest. I know I said that without a trace of ego, for it was nothing but the truth. In a book such as this there could be nothing but the truth; there is no point in trying to obfuscate the facts, they are as they are. It is far too late to attempt any kind of cover-up; there is little point in doing it, I decided. Either I tell the truth, or I don't bother to tell the reader anything. Agreed?

So, even as I questioned the role my family played in my development earlier in this narrative, I have come to see that the Kennedy clan made me every part of what I was. I believed I had made it on my own, for the longest time I thought that way, but writing this out for my readers has given me a clearer insight into the background on which I depended. The motto 'one for all and all for one' completely defined and described the Kennedys far better than any lengthy narrative I have here.

And so I go back to my enrolment as a freshman in Harvard. I felt the sense of history that surrounded the place; I was slightly over-awed by the buildings, by the tutors, by the very fact of being there. That lasted possibly a month, maybe more, maybe less, my memory is somewhat uncertain because of everything that happened after that. It was a relatively short period of time anyway; then the whole scenario of Harvard became familiar, just as any place does when you have been in it for a while and I settled down to get on with my studies. I had friends, I had a good time - and I had girlfriends.

I thought this might be an appropriate moment to talk about the making of John Fitzgerald Kennedy as a ladies' man. I am aware that I actually headed this section 'the political awakening' and here I am speaking about women. Anyone who knew me, anyone who knows of me, would be aware my life was inextricably mixed with women. So, even as I thought on my political development, I could not ignore what I prefer to think of as the 'romantic' side of my life.

The truth is; I loved women. It did not matter whether they came with glowing references for intellect, studiousness or anything else. As far as I was concerned, all they needed in the way of references was a body that I could hold and fondle and lips that I could kiss and arms that were prepared to hold me and not let me go. It meant my studies were far more interesting if I was not sat at a desk aching with sexual frustration, but rather aching from sexual excess. The latter was infinitely preferable to the former. I thought; ask any of the males reading this book at this time whether that is right - see what answer you get. The sexual drive is the most powerful thing the human race has; it overcomes all else. It overcomes common sense, logical thought, moral teaching and just about anything else you can think of which would and should come between the male and female, both of whom appear to be on heat at the same time, in a manner of speaking.

So, if there was one thing I was known for, it was women. Certain names came to the fore each time my name is mentioned, simply because they were/are famous. There were many others, a goodly number of whom are sealed secrets in my heart. They know who they are, I know who they were: some things are not for the world to know. I take the view that the world knows enough already. I had to consider the peace of mind of those women who were good enough to accommodate me, not distribute their name widely to the world. Unfair? Consider this, all ladies who are reading this: what if it was *you* I was talking about? Would you be happy to have your name written into this book for all to know, to gossip about, to have people point the finger and say 'she was another of his conquests'? I doubt very much if any one of you would appreciate that happening.

My decision was made on this point before I began; I knew I would not speak the names of all of those who were good enough to love me. I had decided I would only say I had more than my share. That is not telling the reader something they do not already know, it is confirming what they already know.

How many pages could I absorb in telling you about women? (This is of course before I married.) There are many instances of people trying to analyse why I chased so many women so consistently instead of staying in one relationship. I am quoted as saying I did not know why I was so driven and at the time that was the truth. I needed, for the sake of this book, to sort out my thoughts before I approached the channel to begin work: the sorting out naturally involved questioning my motives back then. It would be unfair of me right now to say I still didn't know and it would not be true, either.

The truth is: I found women irresistible. I loved the secret places of them; I loved the giving flesh, the fact that although anatomically they were all the same, every one of them was very, very different. It never failed to amaze me just how different they were, how they reacted in different ways to the things I did and the things they did. I am not prepared to go into details: if the reader doesn't know, then I advise them to go find their own women and experiment with them. I trust they will have as much pleasure and fun in the research as I did...

I am not entirely sure why I pursued this for so long, except that it was -- being honest, as I had committed myself to be -- a compulsion. I thought I had my share of women about ten times over, going from one to another; not stopping to think what damage might be done emotionally, physically, or even financially. It is only now that the word 'blackmail' comes to mind. I realise I was incredibly lucky not to get involved with someone who would put pressure on the Kennedys because of it. At least, not as far as I knew, anyway. I am sure someone would have told me if it had happened. They told me about everything else. They told me as if I should understand that I should be virtually celibate without accepting or realising that was a physical impossibility for me. For compulsion you could actually read addiction. Having that few moments of utter bliss, of being pain-free, almost equalled the few moments of unbelievable ecstasy that every act of love brought with it. Just how fortunate was I to have two sensations from one moment! No wonder it was addictive. No wonder I gave way to the compulsion time after time after time.

I have decided to return to the topic of my affairs later in the book, in their rightful place, which was alongside the political life I lived. The public will have (nearly) all the information they have wanted for these many years, I believe.

'Just how good am I?' Then I added, 'And you can take that question any way you wish...'

I learned everything I could about the political situation in my country and learned to handle (in a manner of speaking, that is); to be with, to court and then to make love to women. It was quite an education. I found in many respects the two things ran parallel with one another. I have decided to explore this thought.

To court women a man needs a certain diplomatic skill. I could not approach them with crudity, with rough gestures, with an overwhelming ego, even if I came with one. I had to make them believe that they were doing most of the running, that they actually wanted the man more than I wanted them. The subtle art of persuading them they are the one the man wants for the night, maybe even a few days, maybe longer than that, is the carrot is dangled before them and the man had only to wait until the bait was taken. Men have to learn to talk with them on the matters they are interested in, not overwhelm them with their own opinions from the start.

If all goes well, that comes later. Most of all, to treat them with the utmost consideration, even when the man only wishes for the relationship to end. Having a degree of charisma, however anyone identifies that, was a help. I admit I did tend to look upon it all as a game. Without giving it a name, it was very much a game of 'chase', one which I invariably won. Having gained the prize, willing arms and tender body, men then have to work at the pleasure aspect. How much does a man seek his own gratification and how much is he prepared to give to his partner? It should be mutual, it isn't always. But if the man is patient and considerate, he can usually achieve his aim, gratification.

The simple fact is, I did not believe I had very long to live. I knew there were many things wrong with me, some of it unidentified, all of it difficult to cope with and far from easy to relegate to the back of the mind. In the chase, in the conquering, in the ecstasy that came at the conclusion of the chase, there were supreme moments when the pain disappeared. Of course it immediately resurfaced once that moment of ecstasy had faded, but for that blessed short time it was gone. So there were two reasons for my constantly chasing women: one was to constantly relieve myself of the pain, the other was to ensure I had sufficient gratification before the end came. I did not expect the women to love me; I did not expect long-term relationships to come out of any conquests. I knew the woman I wanted to be by my side and I knew I had not met her up to that time. I knew she was out there in the world somewhere; it was just a matter of time before I did meet her and made her my own.

And then there was the political side of my life.

Once someone has an understanding of the political situation in the United States, once they have made up their minds whether they are a Democrat or a Republican, they then begin to play the party game.

They learn to glad-hand those who share the same political beliefs, they learn to make small talk that conveys hidden messages which the other person always manages to understand; they learn to make themselves accessible for any role that is going in the party so they can increase their standing with those who matter. That is, those who will eventually offer their backing for someone to become a congressman. For a long time I looked no further than that. On the outside, that is. Inside, in the secret thoughts that Jack Kennedy kept to himself, I knew I wanted to go all the way to the top. I did not fully appreciate the difficulties this would give me, the struggle it would be, the sheer exhausting campaigning it would involve, but I knew I wanted it. Not everyone nurses a secret ambition. Many are content with what life gives them, they look for no more than sufficient money to live on, a comfortable home, a good companion and partner, children to carry on their name and a few friends. Some seek no more than to escape the poverty trap. Some seek no more than to break out of the racial divide and become accepted by the world. Some seek no more than to leave their own country, cross the border and come into the USA. It is my experience all the people I mentioned are the majority.

Then there are those who seemed to carry a flame inside them, a burning desire to do much, much more than that. It is from within that group that the great artists, musicians, composers, writers, singers, actors and leaders come. Every one of these individuals started out with a desire to be different. More than that, to be outstanding, for only by being outstanding can their talent be noticed by others. Only when the talent is noticed by others can they make progress in their chosen fields. A writer needs to find the right publisher for an outstanding book so that they can be noticed and published and brought to the attention of the public. A musician or singer will need to find the right person to listen to their demo disc. A leader must begin to make his mark on the world in the lower ranks of a political party, working his or her way to the top, carefully, step by step. If they are fortunate, as I was, to have the backing of a family which had prestige, wealth and influence, it is so much the better for them. Having said that, I am aware there have been many outstanding leaders who have come from extremely poor families and made it by their own efforts. They are to be applauded. I was one of the fortunate ones. That is not to say my political career was handed to me on a plate. I had to work for it. I believe I would have been a lesser leader if it had been handed to me, if there had been no struggle, for it is in overcoming obstacles that people grow in stature, experience and understanding.

So the reader will see me at this time, a young man already having had a lot of sexual experience, a lot of pleasure and a considerable amount of ill health, still looking for the right woman and indeed the right direction for his life.

And so the reader sees me, this young man, coming from a politically minded family, having had a first-rate education, uncertain about many things, wanting and ready to explore the 'unknown' world.

Europe.

Travelling Days

When John Fitzgerald Kennedy toured Europe and learned so much

Imagine this: a convertible, a desire, a friend, Lemoyne Billings, and Europe opening up for me and my friend. Kennedy name, Kennedy connections, Kennedy influence meant that, politically, Europe was wide open and waiting.

We went on the *SS Washington*, a luxurious ship, a great way to start a journey. I recall we had a smooth crossing, scarcely a ripple on the surface, not that we spent much time looking over the side, as after a while an endless stretch of water becomes monotonous. Instead we sampled the delights of the cruise ship, including such women as were available. It was not possible for either of us to go very long without female companionship... fortunately neither of us found it difficult to interest the women we met. In a very short time friendships had been created which lasted until the ship docked in France. Addresses were exchanged with promises of ongoing contact, both sides knowing it would not happen. It was just something we had to do.

The convertible was unloaded onto dry land and the two men, full of energy from the constrictions of the ship, anxious and ready to immediately begin their journey through France, disembarked and set off.

Everything was different, landscape, buildings, people, food and of course language. We were welcomed everywhere we went, which pleased us very much. I liked France a good deal. I felt there was an elegance in the buildings, the larger ones that is, and I acquired a liking for what I thought of as the stocky little farmhouses and outbuildings, so different from those I was used to on the American ranches. I also liked the way the French lived, cafes which spilled onto the street where I and my friend would sit for ages and watch the people by whilst we drank good coffee or red wine. I thought there was both an air of affluence about the place and an air of optimism, too. I was not sure, though, why I thought the optimism was misplaced. At the time I kept the thought to myself.

From France the plan was to go through Italy, Germany and Holland and then cross the Channel to England. We stayed in France for about a month, taking the opportunity to talk to Consulate staff and many other people, anyone we could talk to, getting a real feeling of the place and the political situation. Then we moved on.

I found Germany entirely different. I did not find the buildings to be so elegant; they were more utilitarian in their appearance and seemed to represent the rather brash face that the Germans were showing to the world at that time. They were most welcoming, I have to say and we were entertained everywhere we went. We had a very good time. I thought, even at this distance of time, the differences between the two countries were extremely obvious. Although I was welcomed, I did not feel quite as relaxed with the Germans as I had with the French. I also detected undertones to many of the conversations, an ambivalence which was difficult to quantify. I decided to shelve the thought and wait, to observe, to allow the future to show me what I was actually seeing and feeling.

I have just looked at that sentence and thought that it was extremely strange and yet it summed up perfectly what was happening at the time. I knew what I was seeing and feeling, I knew what I was sensing from the undercurrent of conversations, but I could not put any of it together in a form which anyone else would understand. I knew if I waited long enough, it would reveal itself. The future would show me what I was thinking at that time. There, I thought, it really does make perfect sense.

Italy I found to be flamboyance, ancient beauty, with a richness of art and sculpture and with welcoming and friendly people, combined with almost a seeming indifference to the rest of the human race. It was as if being Italian was enough for them, they had no time or place for anyone else. They had a great love for their country, its art, its culture, its rich colourful countryside and I could easily see the attraction. I would have liked to have lingered there a good deal longer than I did. There was an air about the place, not necessarily the weather, but the ambiance, the almost disconcerting way in which the Italians lived cheek by jowl with their ancient monuments and traditions. The oddly costumed Vatican guards were of great interest, the Vatican itself drew me, Catholic as I was, by what it stood for as much as the overwhelming opulence. To make a study of it would have taken years, time I did not have, for this was to be a tour rather than a concentrated visit to one place. I promised myself if I had the chance, I would go back.

Holland was flat, industrious, the windmills, the dykes and the canals. The busy efficient Dutch, bustling about their lives, were a tremendous contrast to the Italians, who seemed to have a greater zest for life. I was aware that this was almost a cliché but it was the impression I got and could not shake it. I liked the people very much; I liked the country too but had no real plans to return to view it again. I did not think I would find anything new to observe, whilst hoping that I was wrong.

At this time I was only a young man on my first trip to Europe and I was putting down on paper the impressions that I gained on that very first visit. My friend Lem agreed with me, saying he saw things the same way as I did, but I did not know how much of that was real and how much of it was just being polite to a travelling companion who had provided the car and the opportunity to go. I hope I am not denigrating the memory of a very fine friend, but this book has to be my feelings, my truthful feelings and nothing else. I admit that I could not have chosen a finer companion for my first trip to the Continent. Lem, dear friend, that is the truth, you know that where you are concerned, I do not lie.

Were there women on the journeys? You need to ask? Of course there were. I soon realised one thing; it was not always my name, my family, which brought women into my arms and my bed, but me. That was a revelation indeed, for though I made many conquests in the USA – and I mean many - I often asked myself whether I or my brother's reputation had been the reason for them seemingly being attracted to me. To go to another country, one that was on the other side of a very large ocean, where the name was not as well known, to find I had the same effect on them, made a great impression on me. I confess that it added tremendously to my ego. But I believe the reader knew that anyway...

Looking back over what I have just written, I thought it seemed to be almost simplistic. The countries and their people were almost stereotypes, which bothered me a lot at first. Not the fact that I had written them that way, but the fact I saw them that way. The French with their street cafes, the Germans with the utilitarian buildings, the Italians with their art and their zest for life, the hard-working Dutch, but the truth is that is the way I saw them - at that time. I could not change the impressions I gained from that tour. What else I absorbed is revealed in my book *'Why England Slept.* . Politically, I felt that each country was many miles away from its neighbour in its outlook. I was aware that France feared Germany, because of its extra strength in many directions, I felt that Holland was very much on the edge of this 'alliance' and sometimes feared for itself and its security and I really did feel Italy did not take any of them seriously.

And then we went to England.

My first impression was how small everything was. The port seemed too small for the amount of shipping docking there, the amount of passengers disembarking there, the amount of transport needed to take those passengers away. And yet it worked. Lem and I and the car disembarked and drove onto English roads with the minimum of difficulty. It felt as if we had hardly begun to travel when we arrived at a large town, a village, somewhere. There was no sense of vast open spaces, something we had gotten used to travelling through France and Germany.

London was crowded, jammed with historic buildings, museums, art galleries, elegant expensive hotels and every tourist attraction I could think of. I wanted to experience it all; I wanted to visit every museum, every beautiful church, to see every painting and every sculpture, but there was only so much time to allocate to this wonderful place. I did my best. Unfortunately there was a need for such things as eating and sleeping, meeting people and other time-consuming activities which got in the way of the real need, to see everything. I promised myself I would return as soon as I could.

The readers are now asking what I was on about. Did I not come to England to study at the LSE? Did I not date women, did I not go about the city, was I not in England? Yes, I was. But the first time I went straight to London from the USA, I went to the LSE and enrolled, I did 'student' things. Arriving in Dover from the continent was entirely different. It was as if I had come to a completely different place. I now realise that it was because I had a totally different mindset from the first time I was there. I went as a student, found that the college was not to my liking, spent a great deal of time drinking and cavorting, there is no other word for it and, I have to admit, being extremely unwell as I was at that time and somehow did not get any sense of what London was all about. It could well have been the companions I had which influenced me. I do not know for sure, all I know is that on this journey I saw England --and London -- with completely different eyes and as I had vowed to do nothing but tell the truth, this is the truth.

Certainly there was a greater appreciation of art and sculpture and buildings on this trip than before. I was actually reluctant to leave.

What I did become aware of, something which I had not noticed on my earlier visit; was the island mentality. It was as if the Channel was a huge barrier stopping anyone and anything reaching the shores. This I found strange in view of the inordinate amount of people who had crossed the water and invaded the country, Vikings to Normans and onwards. And yet it was as if the barrier was real. Any mention of rearmament by other countries was met with a blank look and the reassurance that nothing would touch the British. It was extremely difficult to convince them there were undercurrents across Europe which would bring their own problems if they were not confronted. No one seemed prepared to listen. I could do no more than leave them in their bubble of faith that nothing would touch them. It was with this in my mind that I finally returned to the USA and what I thought of as normal life.

What I had seen, heard, discussed and felt stayed with me. I wrote many notes, many, many notes, believing that one day I would need to use them. In fact they stood me in good stead when I returned to England a year or so later with my father, because I could refer to them and make my decision on how to deal with politicians, using what I had already discovered and from what was happening when they got there.

But that is for another section.

Before then it was back to the usual routine, class, girls, parties: everything a young man needed to do!

European Days

*When John Fitzgerald Kennedy lived in England and
toured the continent - again*

This time it was different. This time I came to England
with my father and brother. We sailed on the *SS
Normandie* in June 1938 and I spent some time working
with my father, who had been appointed US ambassador
to the Court of St James'. We came with credentials,
with a task and, as far as I was concerned, with an open
mind. I was not entirely sure that my father came with an
open mind; he was rather set in his ways by then. I did
not know what my brother Joe was feeling or thinking;
there were times when we did not discuss such things. I
did not know to this day whether Joe was pleased or
displeased with my accompanying them to England.

I spent July working at the embassy, helping to deal
with much of the paperwork which seemed to
accumulate in the office of the US ambassador. I was not
entirely sure how so much paperwork could be generated
by one office. But that's me looking back on it now: at
the time it seemed highly reasonable that the ambassador
should be busy from morning to night with loads of
paperwork which had to be read, discussed, dictated and
signed. There seemed to be endless meetings, much
rushing off here and there, usually in the embassy car
which was at our disposal, all of it time-consuming and
some of it incredibly boring. The one thing I learned
when on a diplomatic posting anywhere was to keep a
bland face and an air of interest, even if I was bored out
of my skull. I also had to know how to compartmentalise
the information I received, to store names and put them
to faces and to be very careful not to commit any
indiscretions such as passing on snippets of information
which should not travel from one person to the other. I
held as my mantra 'if in doubt, say nothing.' It worked
very well.

In August, the Kennedys as a family went to the villa in Cannes. It was a relief to be away from London, to be able to relax and be ourselves, without the constrictions of the diplomatic world on all that we did, said and thought. In my later years as a politician, I would think back to that time and wonder why I got involved in politics. That may sound foolish coming from someone who held the highest office in the world - and you have to believe it was an honour beyond honours for me to be so appointed - but 'goldfish bowl' has nothing on political life, especially when you are President. Even in my early days as a congressman, when I was aiming to go higher, I realised how intrusive the world is for those who would serve in this way.

I wonder how many politicians, for all their positions of power and wealth that goes with it, would wish to the other ends of the earth all political commentators, paparazzi, fellow politicians - the list is endless. I thought: you can count on one hand the activities you can do without someone watching you, photographing you, recording every word, filming you for posterity. Here is where I launch into whimsical thoughts: are they not envious of your power, your wealth and resent the fact they have to be servile to you and have to obey your every word? Those who are chosen to guard, those who are supposed to lay down their life for you, are no more than paid minions. I do not denigrate their loyalty but at the root of most loyalty lies hard cash. I had no illusions about those who surrounded me at all times. In their hearts they were probably Republicans, but even if they were Democrats, it made little difference. They were paid to guard, they did not do it from love, loyalty, friendship, devotion, or any other word you wish to put there. Do I sound cynical? If I do, apologies. What I am trying to do here is not only give the reader an insight into my life, but the life of any president who holds the position. The current incumbent has a greater fear for his life than any preceding him. I actually feel intensely sorry for him; he has a task beyond the ability of any human being; he is trying to do the impossible. He is doing it against a background of racial hatred which runs deep in the American psyche and will be many generations in the eradication. I thought, President Obama must be fully aware every time he leaves the White House there is someone waiting to kill him. The Secret Service is surely more than aware of the fact; that goes without saying. But are they competent? Am I casting aspersions? I suggest anyone who thinks I am should take a look at the short piece of film of the time when someone took a shot at President Reagan. The Secret Service men around him failed to see the gunman, they were all taken by surprise when shots rang out and anyone can see from the film that every one of them was looking in a different direction. They had no idea what was going on. I have to believe, for President Obama's sake, they have improved over the years. If they have, shame that it was too late for me.

I did not plan such a diversion. I realised, however, half way through dictating it, it was something I had wanted to say for a very long time. I would not have dared to have uttered such words during my presidency; the reader can imagine how well that would have gone down! I have had the best part of fifty years on the other side of life to observe the presidents who followed me into office, not only the presidents but all who served them in all capacities. The White House is overloaded with staff, all of whom appeared to have essential jobs to do and, I admit, the place ran like clockwork. I have to return to my main thought, though, how many were there out of loyalty and how many because it was employment? I knew my true friends and advisers at the time, nothing I have seen since my abrupt departure from life has changed my opinion on those people. I chose well in those I nominated to high positions, none of them failed me, as far as I was concerned anyway. I have to hope that each incumbent after me chose equally well. It is not easy to choose someone who will serve you as you wish based on friendship and trust, because the office of President puts up a barrier between you and those whom you have entrusted with friendship. The only way I can put up an analogy here is to say it is like somebody Royal marrying a commoner and they then becoming Royal. That immediately puts them on a different standing with their family, friends and the public. Exactly the same thing happens when someone takes the presidential oath. They are no longer the same person. For better or worse, they are immortalised as the XXth president of the United States of America and they can never again return to normal life.

I think I have gone on long enough. It is time I returned to my life story.

It was around Christmas 1938 when I really became aware of the rumbling undercurrents across Europe. It was apparent in the conversations we had when attending diplomatic parties, meetings, even casual conversations over coffee or lunch with chance-met acquaintances often set all my antennae quivering. I told my father I needed to learn more and he said the only way to learn anything was to go out there among the people and talk with them.

That is what I did. After a lot of planning, discussions and telephone calls, I embarked on a serious, intensive tour of Europe, the Balkans, the Soviet Union and a good deal of the Middle East. For eight months I criss-crossed the countries, using my name to get into conversations with those in the know, going back to hotel rooms or occasionally the homes of those I had talked with and there wrote my extensive notes. For the most part I wrote the facts, on other sheets, though, I wrote my feelings.

My intention was to gather information and impressions for my senior honours thesis at Harvard as well as get a feeling for what was going on. That was the aim: what actually happened was I became deeply involved with the whole political scene enacted across those countries. The differing views, the entrenched positions, the long-held prejudices, all contributed to what I thought of – and felt - as the boiling mass of trouble about to explode. It was clear that these countries could not live in harmony with one another, for there were imbalances of indigenous supplies, of skilled and unskilled labour, of both short sighted and farsighted leadership and last but far from least the level of corruption evident everywhere I went. The atmosphere in Europe had changed completely since my first trip. Then I had not really been aware of barriers and borders, this time they were very evident, especially in the militancy of those manning checkpoints. They perused documents far more thoroughly, asked searching questions, they even wanted to look in my car to find what I might be carrying. They almost seemed disappointed when they found nothing. I spent a good deal of time talking with consulate staff and diplomats at all levels, to get a sense of the overall political situation. Nothing that I heard encouraged me to think there would be any way that Europe could avoid confrontation. The one thing that did surprise me was the way people spoke so freely on all the topics which I raised. I didn't expect them to do that. I thought people would be circumspect about military matters, diplomatic discussions, how they personally felt about the impending conflict, but they were not. And because of this I was able to gather a good deal of information which I had not expected to get. This was both pleasing and worrying, because it meant they placed a great reliance on me. I wasn't sure whether they expected me to take a leading role in negotiations, or to report back as accurately as I could, or quite what was in their minds. Later, when thinking about it, I wondered if they just needed to unload that which was worrying them and I happened to be a good listener. Whatever the reason, I gained great insight and later I took all this information back first to England and then to the United States.

The prospect of war was unsettling, upsetting and frightening. The juggernaut of military supremacy appeared to have been set in motion and no one seemed capable of stopping it. My feeling was no one wanted to stop it. Some of this I wrote down, the rest I kept in my heart, not wanting to commit it to paper. I was ostensibly on a fact finding mission, I had to show that was my purpose, so as not to upset those who were clearly edgy and looking for reasons to stop me getting through the checkpoints. That in turn made me wonder what they had to hide.

During the journeying I was fawned over as an American but only insofar as I was possibly able to supply something for them, such as information, contacts, advice (although quite where they thought someone of my age would be able to find such a commodity was quite beyond me) and, in some instances, direct links to criminal organisations which could supply them with weapons, trucks, drugs, even slaves. 'People trafficking' was the most common activity and the one which upset and worried me the most. I also quickly learned 'Indentured servants' was a metaphor for slavery. I thought; if people do not believe that slavery still exists in this world, then they are blind to what is really there.

It took me a while to come to terms with the many requests made for these things. Sometimes they came from the men at the top, sometimes from minions further down the food chain, but I never went anywhere without requests made for something which I was unable to supply, even if I wanted to.

I had believed that my character was set at this point, that there was little I would wish to change about myself, but this odyssey, I could think of it in no other way, revealed a deep humanitarian streak I was not aware I possessed. The journey, the experiences, set me against all racial prejudice for a start. When someone becomes aware of ethnic minorities exploited as virtual slave labour and spoken of, in some instances, with virulent hatred, it had an effect. This, coupled with everything I learned politically, gave me a considerable amount to think about when I returned to my family and finally went back to the United States. I concluded my odyssey a much wiser person than when I started.

I got back on the 1st September 1939, just as Germany invaded Poland. I did not know the invasion was that close. I had not believed it would be too long before Germany pushed across her borders and into other lands, but I did not think it would be that soon. I experienced a great rush of relief and then immediately felt guilty for that. Then I realised I really was very grateful to be out of it. That sounds selfish when written down, I thought, but then I ask, if it were you, would you not feel the same way?

All this political thought and information, everything I had learned, felt and observed, culminated two days later when I sat with my father in the Strangers Gallery of the House of Commons, listening to the debates supporting the declaration of war against Germany. It was a pivotal moment for me. It was one thing to be aware of a war about to break out, another thing entirely to be present when the government of one of the combatants actually declares a state of war. It was chilling, to say the very least. On those words hung the lives of hundreds and thousands of people.

I wondered how many people realised that. I believed Winston Churchill did, but did others? I found the experience highly emotional as well as revealing. I also realised that all of this, every experience, resonated with me in some way. I became more empathetic even to the point of being in disagreement with my father over the survivors of the British destroyer which had gone down. The surviving American citizens were in Glasgow, pleading for an escort to take them back to the States. They were terrified. I would have been surprised if they hadn't been, but my father didn't see it that way. He thought they were making a fuss. All I could do was offer the meagre reassurance that President Roosevelt and the embassy were convinced that the Germans wouldn't attack a US ship. Paper promises. Weak convictions. These people had been thrown into the sea. A hundred people had died, some of them US citizens. And there I was, on my father's instructions, trying to say 'it won't happen to a US ship.' I wondered how I could say such a thing; how I could make anyone else believe such a thing, when they had been through such a terrifying ordeal. I had no choice, no one was prepared to authorise an escort as everything was geared to the war in Europe. It looked as if the USA was standing back from it and letting the British get on with it, in some ways. I knew there were good reasons for it, the USA's lack of rearmament for one thing.

It is impossible for me to describe in my book how it felt for me to send those people back on an unescorted ship while I went by air. I went in total guilt and remorse that I had not done more, had not been able to do more, that I had not been in a position to do more.

They went in fear. I went in luxury and safety.

The privilege of class and wealth.

Sometimes it hammered itself into my conscious mind and stuck there like a large thorn.

Sometimes I lived with it and did not think about it.

Sometimes I was damned glad it was there.

Uncertain Days
How John Fitzgerald Kennedy spent the pre-war years

Throughout my flight back to the USA, I suffered a sense of guilt that I had allowed the survivors to go home on yet another ship. I realised the thought was foolish, there was nothing else I could have done. My father had not authorised me to do anything else and I was bound by that. It did not stop me feeling guilty. The traumatised people deserved better. Being privileged did not make easier to for me to cope with it. One day, I told myself, one day I will be in a position of power, then no one dare tell me what I can and cannot do. If I want to provide escorts and security for American citizens, I will! The determination made me feel a little better, but it was a long time before the guilt left me.

Back in the USA, I began putting together all the thoughts, notes and impressions, everything I had gained from my tour around Europe, having decided to use it as a thesis for my degree. Why not, I thought. I had worked really hard to get the information, the extensive travelling, the extensive consultations, the extensive observations, all combined to make one very potent thesis, or so I thought. I worked at it, talked about it, drove everyone mad with it – deciding that was their problem, not mine - and finally it all came together in a form which pleased me, at least. There were criticisms, of course there were, I would have been surprised had it been universally accepted. The fact was I had worked hard to get the information and worked equally hard to put it together in the thesis, so when the degree was given to me I knew I had earned it. I was proud of the finished product, knowing there were few who could have presented such a comprehensive picture of the impending conflagration, which by then was occupying a good deal of everyone's attention.

The content surprised a good many people, but what was more surprising to me was the suggestion the thesis became a book. I had no intention of doing such a thing at that time; it really was work for the thesis and no more, apart from giving me a background for my occasional diplomatic duties. But the more I thought about it the more I liked the idea. Certainly there was a great deal in everything I had written which would be food for thought for senators and others alike to appreciate the current situation in the world. So I put it together as a manuscript.

The first publisher turned it down. A second company turned it down but the third took it and, to my great surprise, 'Why England Slept' became a bestseller. Who would have thought that a treatise on disarmament and rearmament would sell! It was not the stuff of bestsellers in normal circumstances. But of course, the times were not normal. War was raging in Europe and those in the States were standing back to watch what was going to happen so that they could decide which way they were going to go. That sounds very cold but it was nothing more than the truth. Diplomatically and politically it was extremely difficult to work out the appropriate stance. The USA needed to support their allies, but they also had their own problems to confront at the time. What was surprising about the sales of the book was this: it was not a life story, it was not scandalous, it used the Kennedy name but at that time I was not that well known. Had I put this book out when I became president, I would have expected great sales for it, simply because of who I was. I had to assume, from the unexpected success of it, that people were genuinely interested in the subject rather than the author and that in itself was a great compliment. Even now I remain proud of the book and have been reading it again; thinking there was nothing I would change if I were given the chance to rewrite it now. It is a good feeling; to be so proud of a piece of writing that after all these years I could still read it and think; 'I did a good job.'

After gaining my degree, I felt at a loose end for a while, a period combined with not being very well (again). I did some work at the Stanford Graduate School of business on the basis of my degree; helped my father write his book on his time as ambassador and went to a conference on the subject of world affairs where I was able to make a contribution. The ongoing war bothered me a great deal. My first-hand experience of the militancy of Germany had made me very aware of the major threat they posed. It was almost beyond belief, to me, that others did not see the same threat. Perhaps they expected France, Belgium, Holland and the Baltic states to defend themselves so strongly that the German army would be driven back beyond its own borders. I knew well this was not going to happen. Many had not re-armed, simply because their leaders were either too afraid to order re-armament or there simply was not sufficient money to do it. In times of crisis, I thought, money has to be found for arms. In many cases it was too late, anyway. Germany simply crossed the borders and took possession where they could.

I soon found other people were not as interested as me in what was happening in the rest of the world. It was as if the war was not happening. I found this extremely puzzling, it put me at odds with a lot of people, such as those who did not wish to listen to the news as avidly as I did, those who did not have enough grasp of what was going on to be able to discuss it with me. This resulted in my feeling somewhat on the periphery of life. It was a feeling I became used to, simply because more times than not I was the odd one out. It didn't help very much that time proved the rightness of my arguments, some people remembered and admitted they were wrong, others had dismissed the discussions and I did not revive the memory, for people have a selective memory when it comes to things they do not wish to remember. In doing that, I was already practising diplomacy, was I not? If they would not listen, there was nothing anyone could do to enlighten them.

I travelled extensively in South America.

These are comparatively disparate things and so, anyone looking at them from a distance of time would conclude, as I did, that Jack Kennedy was not sure which way he wanted to go. Travelling was always good; the welcome opportunity to see new places, new faces and to garner new facts. The problem was - unless someone was an international journalist or something of that kind, travelling was not a good way to make a living. I did not appreciate at the time that what I was desperately doing was working out a way to find a foundation on which to build a future. I have already mentioned the constant moves as a family, the fact I had no room of my own, moving from university to university, from country to country and all the travelling I had done did nothing to help me find my roots, my foundation, the blocks on which I wanted to build. The success of my thesis-cum-book put the idea in my head that I could attempt journalism, but somehow it did not appeal to me as it should. I knew I really needed to be committed to that kind of life and I was not fully able to commit myself. I did have thoughts about renewing my application to Yale, but it was only a thought.

Then I was called up by the Army - and was refused. They took one look at my medical record, looked at me, asked a few questions and told me I was rejected. I argued with them, but they said with a back as bad as mine and a stomach condition as bad as mine, there was no way they could allow me to be part of the armed forces. Although I expected it, it still came as a terrible blow for I felt as if I should be doing something. The family were sympathetic but unhelpful. What could they have done about it? The Army said no, so it was no.

So there I was, rejected on the grounds of health, not knowing where I wanted to go or what I wanted to do. It came at a bad time; I was already unsure of my future and then to have the Army reject me ... it was something which many people would have been grateful for, but not me. For one thing I didn't want everyone to know the extent of my illness, this was after all a private battle between my body and me and for another thing, it would not do for a Kennedy to be seen to be opting out of anything to do with the war. My father was already attracting criticism for his appeasement stance, my brother was a Navy pilot, what would people have said if I had walked away and taken a place in a law school or something safe like that? It would not have looked good. More than that, it was not good for me. I needed to have my self-confidence boosted and it would not happen if I allowed myself to be sidelined out of the armed forces at a time when part of the world was at war. Regardless of what anyone said, I knew that the USA would become involved in the war sooner or later. How and where and to what degree was beyond my knowledge, I just knew it was going to happen. If I became involved and was killed, at least I would go out in a blaze of glory. The thought of dying in a war did not disturb me; the simple fact was I already believed that I did not have a long life ahead of me because of my serious health conditions.

It was only later when I was elected to the office of President that I began to realise my life was very likely to be cut short by an outsider. But again, that was something I learned to live with. It is in fact something every president learns to live with. The Secret Service personnel know this and spend their entire existence working to avoid just that happening. They weren't always successful... if they had been, the Kennedy family members would have had longer lives than they did. This is not a criticism: it is an observation. If someone is determined to kill you, they will do it regardless of how many secret service men you have around you. I was proof of that, leaving aside the idiocy of travelling in an open top car, of course...

The reader is entitled to ask: what was the real, the heart-felt reason I pursued a career in the armed forces when I could have walked away. They are entitled to know, but – I am not sure I know myself what it was. Was it courage? Was it courage combined with patriotism, or was it what my conscience told me it was, a desire to Show Father That I Was As Good As Joe any day of the week? Having written that out, I am inclined to say that was the real reason. Joe's death and my becoming a war hero were coincidental to the original reason for going. Neither of those events was foreseen. Losing my brother might have been, but the 'it won't happen to us' feeling held the family together, believing that our prayers, fervent and emotional as they were, would keep Joe safe.

They didn't. It was very hard on all of us.

It was as if one was taken away and then another given the opportunity to become a hero and make up for it. I don't know. It just looks that way from my perspective now. At the time it was just something I did because I had to do it.

But before then...

My mother and sister were going to Latin America, so I went with them. It was an opportunity to do something different and I went, partly to distract myself from the thoughts which were tumbling around my head at that time, thoughts such as:

I should be part of the fighting forces in the event of the USA being drawn into the European war.

I really should be doing something useful with my life.

I could not keep expecting Father to employ me in this role or another, all the while resenting my body which, on the outside, looked perfectly normal and was still attracting its share of females whilst inside it caused me considerable havoc and discomfort.

With my chronic back condition sometimes it was hard to walk. It was difficult to cope with the restrictive diets and more than that, the appalling effect food had on my stomach and the rest of me, coping with the endless investigations that were humiliating, embarrassing, intrusive, painful, downright awful and mostly got me nowhere, as in - no answers to what was wrong. I was a physical wreck and yet, every day I went to my bed, or if already in bed (a hospital one, more often than not) waiting for sleep, I would think, 'it's been a good day – because I'm still alive, against all the odds. There might be something for me yet, if I live long enough.' God was good enough to answer that prayer, I did get somewhere, I did live long enough, but at times it was a close run thing, especially during the war years.

I looked on it as a battle, the body against 'me'. I had to admit that the body won more times than I did, but it was not for want of trying. What my body had to accept was that I had made a vow that it would not stop me, the person inside, from doing what I wanted with my life.

My body and my spirit carried on the unequal battle until the day of my death.

So I went to Latin and South America with my mother and sister and I left them to travel on my own, going to Argentina, Brazil, Chile, Uruguay, Peru, Ecuador, Colombia and Panama. I came back with memories of extraordinary, extreme, unbelievably beautiful scenery, forests and mountains, lakes and vast plains, with the sound of many languages and dialects ringing in my ears, the incredible range of colours, costumes, houses, flowers; a veritable kaleidoscope of impressions.

Even taking into account the fact that I went to these countries using the Kennedy name and Kennedy wealth, I did manage to see a good deal as a tourist, one who was looking beyond the scenery and the souvenirs to make some effort to understand what was at the heart of the different lives. I saw poverty at a level I could not have believe existed, had I not seen it with my own eyes. It was the kind of thing which I felt I could not learn from TV programmes or documentary films shown in the cinema. These days the world has the History Channel and the Discovery Channel and goodness knows what else available at the touch of what people call a remote. The problem is they are voyeurs; they look at poverty and conflict from the comfort of a sofa in front of a screen which shows them moving pictures. Should they find the pictures too much, they are at liberty to turn off the TV and go and get themselves a drink or something to eat. They can find a book, they can leave the house and take a walk or drive, they can visit friends, or if that is too strenuous, they can change channels. The people I saw did not disappear when I looked away, when I turned back they were still there. The poverty I looked at with appalled horror could not be tackled by the wealth my family had, were they to give away their last dime. To rectify people's lives, a massive change of heart would be needed by those in charge of the country. Unfortunately, as with most leaders, they put their own comfort before their people.

I had no idea at the time how valuable all this travelling and observation would be. There have been Presidents who have not known where countries are in relation to other countries and I admit that if I were asked about Africa, I would be in some difficulty. That continent is one great mass of individual countries, each with their own cultures, rituals, hatreds, tribal loyalties and, most of all, needs. It would take a lifetime to come to terms with each of them. I was grateful and glad that I spent time touring Europe and Latin and South America, for that gave me a good basis and understanding of how different everyone is and how important it was to recognise that each nationality had its own requirements, which may well conflict with others. If more politicians understood that, there would be fewer problems in the world, I believe. So many of them came to office with preconceived ideas on what other people should be looking for, rather than what they are actually looking for. There is a big difference and in that difference is the potential for problems.

I am aware that once again I have launched into a diversion, one leading me away from my life story, but which fits perfectly with my chosen stance on this book, which is to tell the reader how I felt and not what I did. I have to tell the reader what I did so that I can relate how I felt about it, if that makes sense, but what the reader is not going to get is a line by line description of each country, who I met there, my impressions of it, from a tourist point of view that is, but what I brought away with him. For that is the essence of travelling, what you bring away with you. What I brought back from Latin and South America I have related here. I had in my travelling added extensively to my knowledge of other people and that, anyone would say, is a most valuable asset for someone in the political life. The interesting thing is, at that point I had no idea I was going to enter the political arena. I really did not know what I was going to do. The only thing that was a certainty was that I could not waste my life; and I had to do something useful. The burning question was: what?

War Years
John Fitzgerald Kennedy in uniform

After a good deal of deliberation, I made up my mind I had to get into the Armed Forces somewhere and applied to become a Marine. It satisfied me on several levels, not least of which was the fact I already knew how to sail. I thought that might be a useful skill my commanding officers could make use of. I knew my medical record would go against me, but I also knew that if I bribed enough people - I use the word advisedly - I would be able to get in. I blatantly used Kennedy influence to get the position which then led to my determination that they would not regret the appointment, that they would not find me a freeloader, there for the uniform and kudos, but someone who was prepared to work. It was extremely important this was clearly understood and it would only be understood by example, my example, my commitment to the Marines and any men I was associated with. From that the reader will realise that in many ways, PT 109 was inevitable, insofar as my heroics were concerned...

I assume that the world would like some thoughts on PT 109. There's a very good book out there on the subject, with all the gory details, if you really want them. As I said before, this book is not about facts; it's about feelings, emotions and the truth as I saw it.

Truth is like honesty, no two people see it the same way.

Truth is like an image, a view, stand two people in front of it and they will see two very different things.

Everyone sees things according to their own upbringing, principles, ideals and whichever mood they are in at a given moment. There will be people who will read this book who will come back to my channel and say 'this was not Jack Kennedy! He did not have these thoughts! We knew him well. This is not him.' Long before those comments reach my channel – and I know they would if I did not intervene before then – I wanted to say here and now, forget even trying to say them. You may think you knew me well, you may think you knew what I would say, what I would think, what I would do about any given topic at any given moment. The chances are you would be right. I would like you to take a second look at that sentence and see which word is missing from it. The word that is missing is 'feel.'

The only person who knew how I felt about any part of my life, no matter which part was being discussed, was me.

But before then... joining the Marines. My father approved, as far as he approved of anything that did not, in some way or another, impinge on the vision, the shining example, that was my brother Joe.

Viewed from the outside, the Kennedy world was one of a close-knit clan. In many ways it was. Within the family group, apart from the constant competitiveness, there was a singular lack of that most basic of emotions, love. It was not a word we spoke to one another, which leads me now to wonder if it actually existed between any of us for a long time. I had a great deal of affection for my sister Rosemary, she being disabled and needing a good deal of care and attention, but as far as the others were concerned, I thought we were engaged in too much competition with one another to offer any kind of affection. Until I had a home of my own, a wife and family, somewhere to come home to, someone to care for me, I did not appreciate that I was, in fact, lonely.

This changed when I got into politics and found my brothers were a tremendous help on many levels. I trusted Bobby completely and leaned on him heavily, thankful that he was there. But by then I had the settled home and family and could view things differently.

Becoming a Marine gave me a small insight into companionship, for the Marines were like an extended family. Once you joined you became one of them. Whatever you did, provided it was for the good of the group, you were one of them. It was the first time I truly felt I belonged. Prior to this I had gathered a group around me, especially at school and college, but I was the leader of the group rather than being part of it. It seems a very small difference but it is a large one. I also felt, without any basis for the feeling, that the Kennedy family was pleased with the decision I had made. It was too much to ask they would be proud of me.

Sometimes I wondered why it mattered so much. We were all encouraged to follow our pathway, create their own destiny, so why did it matter whether the family would be proud of me or not? I thought it was probably because everyone needs that approbation from their peers. I knew well that I did. I sought closeness and had separation. I sought affection and found rigid rules and coldness. I sought sibling love and found competition.

Life was one endless battle, family, ill health, 'friends' who tried to outdo me in everything. I was pleased at least to have a best-selling book for others to boast about; at least it gave me a degree of respectability within the ambitious, ever striving family I was born into.

I also want to say again that I really thought, with everything I had wrong with me, that I was destined for a very short life; I did not expect to see my 30th birthday. What do you do when you think your time is short? Cram as much into it as you can. So I did, parties and girls and more parties and even more girls until I fair wore out that part of me. It's a wonder that the medical profession didn't pounce on that as a symptom and deny me any sexual activity, but they didn't, for which I was eternally grateful...

Another diversion I did not expect but I am content to have it there.

Having made up my mind that the Marines would be a good place for me, I had to get past the medical. I freely confess at this point that my father's influence made this possible, with a general fudging of the facts about this troublesome body of mine. I did not know if money changed hands, very likely it did, but whatever means was used, I became a Marine. I was extremely proud to be part of a very fine tradition and extremely grateful for any influence that got me the place I needed. There was a sense of grudging admiration from my father that I had determined to do this and carried it through. The fact I had turned a thesis into what transpired to be a bestselling book had already raised me a notch or two in my father's estimation, or at least I chose to believe this, because I needed to. But my belief was based on the hints and intimations I detected in the way my father spoke with his second son.

I am finding it difficult to convey to the reader the strange family life I led. You would have thought any parent would have been delighted with the progress, the achievements, that Kennedy boys managed, but I know well that Robert and Teddy felt the same as I did, that whatever they did, whatever they achieved, was always overshadowed by anything Joe did. It was like fighting mist, something extremely difficult to do. I felt as if I were to walk into the house and announce I had just won the Pulitzer Prize for literature, the reaction would be 'oh really? That's good,' and my parents would go back to doing what they were doing before I walked in. There is merit in inculcating a sense of competition among the siblings and there is totally ignoring their achievements when gained. But there is little point in labouring this subject, it was a burden I carried at the time and one that persisted until Joe was no longer with us. Then of course they all had his memory to contend with. I also confess gaining the presidency gave me an even greater thrill than it would have done under normal circumstances, that is, if I had come from a 'normal' family, because I had achieved something which my brother may well have done had he lived. For the first time in my existence, I had actually stolen Joe's crown.

I watched with great interest and not a small degree of amusement the moment when President Obama came out to speak to the people on the night he knew he was President. For a moment he stopped and looked up as if overwhelmed by the thought he had actually made it. I empathised with that. My 'moment' came before I walked out to speak to the people, when I sent out first a prayer of gratitude that I had been appointed to high office and second a thought to Joe: thank you for clearing the way. May your shadow now stop dogging my heels.

I thought, I really must stop diverting! But then again, the reader is getting the raw, uncensored JFK. What more could they ask?

So there was I in 1941, pushing papers around in the Intelligence Department of the Marines. There were times during my college days when I was bored, but never as bored as I was during that time. Have you ever thought that you should not wish for something? I wished that something would come along to change my ultra dull six-days-a-week office job.

The saying is, be careful what you wish for. I wanted a change but did not anticipate that Pearl Harbor would be attacked and transform my 9-to-5 boring job to a 24 hour 7 day a week situation. Then I ended up on the night shift and the work was frantic.

Before then, fortunately, my sister Kathleen was able to arrange a variety of social occasions which offset the tedium of work and gave me an opportunity to make one sexual conquest after another. Well, I had to do something or I would have gone out of my mind. That was not what I envisaged when I joined the Marines but really, had I given it any serious thought, it should have occurred to me that having given them what was in fact an 'illegal' bill of health, the authorities would ensure that I was kept away from fighting men, for fear of my medical condition being a liability. That was something I only thought about afterwards.

And at the time there was Inga. It's all there, in the books, in the articles; I am not going into that particular relationship in this book. Just to say it was good while it lasted. That should be enough for any reader. I need to move on and say my treacherous body let me down again. My back, my stomach, you name it, some part of me was giving problems and I was certified unfit for duty. I had to consult a doctor yet again and if there was one thing I hated, it was consulting the doctors. Why did they always insist on prodding and poking and drawing blood and wanting this test and that test? Either they know what is wrong with you or they don't. If they do they should prescribe something, if they don't they should leave you alone. There are limits to how much a person can stand.

It is ironic that I should write such a sentence, because it was indicative of my life at that time and my immediate future. At first I found I was battling my family and all the religion that was being pressured on me at the time - and yes, the phrasing is intentional - and so I applied to go to sea to escape those pressures, only to find myself hemmed in by the rules, regulations and sometimes inconsequential happenings from those in authority. I knew well that the whole PT 109 affair came about through incompetence of those in command. I have never made a secret of this; I do not intend to do so, either.

Whatever the reason, perhaps they were short of personnel at the time; I was granted permission to go to sea. It meant going to a Midshipman's School which I did not mind at first. Then I found it to be rather deadly, but have to admit that at that period of my life I found most things dull, nothing was capturing my attention or engaging my intelligence. In fact, the whole thing was stultifying. I feared my mind would turn to mush if something did not come along to wake me up and present me with a real challenge. And yet I have to say I would still go to bed each night and think I had lived through a good day. This was despite being in constant pain, sometimes having difficulty in walking, because I was still alive, my stomach condition had not brought me to the point when I could not eat anything and would therefore be heading toward the early death which I had envisaged for myself. I was still capable of walking about, albeit slowly, with a supreme effort not to let people know how much it hurt and still the outer body appeared to be attractive enough to the females. As long as it went on doing that, I could see no reason to complain. Well, not many reasons, anyway.

I wanted to pilot one of the PTs. I had seen them, admired them and wanted to be on one of them. Perhaps that was a childish notion in some ways, but they were there, dashing here and there, doing their bit for the war effort. I wanted some of that. It was the same throughout my life, I would see, I would desire, I would work at making it my own.

It could be said that I lived a charmed life. I had the looks (apparently) which were alluring to women, despite my ill-health I had managed to get into one of the armed forces (albeit with a little help from my father) and, having gained that goal, I then proceeded to tackle the next, getting aboard a PT. And I did it. I have to say I never gave a thought at the time to the fact that I could see something or wish to do something and somehow it happened. I just lived it without thinking that there were others who possibly had to work a good deal harder than I did to achieve the same ends.

Going on the PT was a mistake as far as my health was concerned. It put my back in serious jeopardy. The boats did not ride smoothly through the water, they bounced, they hit troughs, they rolled; they did everything imaginable to throw a sailor off his feet and into the bars at each side. It meant that constant pain became constant excruciating pain, but I had no intention of giving in. The training was rough, but I had sailed on many occasions off Cape Cod which had given me a very good background in seamanship. Then I came up against a new burden, a new obstacle, almost a conspiracy. It was very much as if the Marines were saying: 'yes you can be a sailor, but not to any particular degree to assist the war effort. We will leave you as a training officer.' That did not go down well with me. I began a series of requests which were guaranteed to get me nearer to the action. I could have asked my father to help, but he had already done a great deal and so I went over my father's head to my grandfather. He had his own strings to pull, a lot of them, and I was given a commission. This made me very happy until I realised that yes, I had a commission but no, I wasn't getting involved in the war. In fact I was being sidelined into possibly spending the entire time in Panama.

I have to say that Panama is an enchanting place. Under any other circumstances I would have been content to stay there but I wanted to be part of the war effort, in the front line, not at the back. A Kennedy is never at the back when there is action; they are always at the front.

It is about now that the reader would be forgiven for seriously thinking that I was completely insane. I had a chronic back condition, a chronic stomach condition and generally was a walking wreck. That was when I was capable of walking! I had refused an operation; instead I embarked on a series of exercises, most of which gave me even more pain, but which actually did help - eventually. This was of course a return to the simple philosophy by which I was living at that time --I had to be as good as Joe. There was no question that I could turn my (damaged) back on this, but I could have stayed through the rest of the war in the intelligence back room, where I could have nursed my many conditions and not have everything aggravated by boats, heat and all the other things which went into undermining my health. Physically that would have been the perfect solution. Mentally it was a scenario I could not entertain. More than that, it was a scenario I refused to entertain. Foolish, foolhardy, risky, yes all of these things but it was necessary for me to make a stand. I requested an assignment in the South Pacific. By a miracle I got it.

In all, I was in the South Pacific for almost a year and a half. I can honestly say I would not have missed the experience for the world. It opened my eyes to many things, not least the horrors of war and the incompetence of those attempting to run the war. It is not something I want to go into at this time, the thoughts I expressed in the many letters I wrote at the time conveyed my feelings far better than I could now, for they were contemporaneous and this is being written in hindsight. What I would say is it played a great part in my future, experiences such as that do not leave you, I mused; they change you.

The whole different atmosphere of the South Pacific stayed with me for many years, not least the feeling that the American forces were doing irrevocable damage to a very beautiful part of the world. Of necessity there had to be huts, storage, vehicles, boats, but all this was alien and brought its own problems. Of necessity there was interaction with the people who lived there, not all of which was good. War touches and spoils all that it touches, I decided eventually. Unfortunately nothing could be done to obviate that, if the enemy wasn't stopped, the damage would have been even more catastrophic.

Inevitably, the book comes to PT109. I would prefer to ignore this completely, simply because I wish my record to stand for the political work I did and the position I held rather than circumstance contriving to make me a 'war hero'. I well understood that the events were a gift to politicians' PR people; they do so love a hero on which to build an urban legend. But a 'hero' is a person who just happens to be in the right place at the time when something happens, when without thinking they do something 'heroic'. Heroics are rarely planned; they are made by coincidence of timing and events. There are many instances of heroes during the wars this world has suffered, simply because they were there when something happened. That is exactly my story.

I was on board PT109, below decks, when a Japanese destroyer rammed what I thought of as 'my' boat. I rushed up on deck and the first thing which happened was I was thrown against the railings. I remember the excruciating pain that went through my back and thought – I decided to replace my actual words with some which are more polite – damn it, that hurt, what damage has been done to my boat and what the hell happened anyway?

The stupid thing was, I knew exactly what had happened but in those few moments of white pain flaring through me, it was as if memory had been blanked out. It all came rushing back as I hit the water and began frantically searching for my crew members.

A quick count showed me that all those who were able were clinging to the part of the hull which was still afloat, but there were five members whom we had to 'rescue' as it were, a strange idea, as we were all shipwrecked. With two others I swam out to bring the survivors back to the wrecked boat. One thing I recalled at the time was that being in the water somehow helped my back condition; either that or the panic of the time helped blot out the pain, for I did not remember any of it then. I did think my mind was totally concentrated on rescuing all those that I could. There was no way I was going to leave any of them to fend for themselves and probably drown. I swam out to one man, someone we called 'Pappy', and found he had been badly burned and incapable of doing anything. I pulled him back to the hull and got someone else to hold on to him. Once he was safely 'back' I went looking for two more whilst mourning the two I knew had been killed.

At this point I had been in the sea for some time, my back injured yet again, seeing my companions floating in the water, some of them in a far worse condition than I was. What does the more able person do but do their best to rescue them? I remembered little of being cold, waterlogged, exhausted. All I remember was that I rescued those I could and mourned those I could not.

At first we talked, shouting to each other across the wrecked boat. We needed to encourage each other so we joked that a liner was coming by to pick them up, envisioned all the luxuries we would have once on board, or a destroyer where at least we could have hot showers, hot meals and drinks. We laughed once or twice but the laughter soon faded away as time went on. We could not carry on clinging to something that was going to sink at some point and no one seemed to know of our predicament so they could arrange to rescue us. I knew we were not far from a strip of land, or so I told the others, and I also told them that we could do it, provided we set our minds to it. It was going to be a long swim but there was no alternative. By my calculation we had been hanging on to the wreck of PT 109 for something like nine hours in total, long enough for anyone to be treading water, literally. We had to do something.

We set out for the island.

The big problem was Pappy. He was too far gone, no strength, no will, to attempt any kind of swim. I realised the only way to get him to the island was to tow him, just as I had towed him back to the hull in the first instance. The only way to do that was to use my teeth. So I swam, with Pappy's life-jacket clenched in my jaws.

I didn't even think about it, I just did it.

It was an endless time. If it really was only five hours and apparently it was, they were the longest hours I had ever lived through and that is really saying something. I had endured many occasions when I believed that time had literally stood still but none like that interminable lonely swim with my jaw and neck aching to the point when I thought I would never be able to speak or eat again and with my arms aching from the effort of swimming for so long with the additional weight of the man I was pulling. As if I had not enough to deal with, my back decided to protest at the strain I was putting on it. The worst thing, though, was the feeling of being desperately alone, unable to speak to anyone because of my need to hold on to the life-jacket, not able to turn my head very far to see how many others were staying right alongside, resenting every moment I was in the water, wondering if I had miscalculated and we would never reach land. It was a waking nightmare. If I had known it was going to take five hours I wonder if I would have had second thoughts, but then again I doubt it, it would have been criminal simply to let the man drown for the sake of making a bit of an effort. That's what I told myself so that I could keep going. After a while my mind blanked out anyway and there was nothing but the need to keep my jaws shut tight so that I did not let go and allow Pappy to drift away and for my arms to keep moving, propelling me forward and for my back to shut up its constant complaint that it was hurting and did not like what I was doing. The war with my body was ongoing, as relentless as the rescue mission to which I was committed.

They made it, all of them. Once all the survivors were all on 'dry land' as it were, well, even if they were soaking wet, they were able to rest on something solid, I swam back out to try and signal anyone who might be passing. No one responded, so I returned to the island. I knew I passed out several times on the journey back. I retain a distinct memory of regaining consciousness, swimming some more and the feeling of blackness coming over again. I believe I was more or less washed up on the beach. Everyone said they didn't expect to see me again, but like the proverbial bad penny, I insisted on turning up. No one got rid of me that easily!

I really couldn't face going back out again and believe if I had, I would not be relating the story now. I would be on this side of life but no hero! Another crew member went instead, but he came back, having had no response.

After an overnight rest we all swam on to Osalana Island, a neighbouring one, in the hope of finding something that we could eat or drink, to regain our strength. Unfortunately there was nothing. Again we rested and then, with my friend Barney Ross, I swam on again to another island where we found a canoe.

I am very aware that these are facts, not feelings. The problem is, at this moment, I cannot say how I felt. I was physically wrecked, through indulging in a swimming marathon, having blacked out several times and being in absolute agony with my back and stomach which had decided to protest at the lack of food and water. So there was really a sense of detachment from the time. I was not really there; I was not really functioning emotionally, only on a physical level, attempting to work out what to do to save the lives of all who had survived the sinking of PT109. The good thing was we found a canoe, together with water, crackers and candy which I took back to the men, to discover that native islanders had found them and were tending to them. This was magnificent news and I was able to go back to the island and rescue my friend Barney who had remained there and from where I sent the message on a coconut which then became quite famous in its own right. Whoever would have thought a coconut would become a relic! I carved in the shell:

NAURO ISL COMMANDER NATIVE KNOWS POS'ITI CAN PILOT 11 ALIVE NEED SMALL BOAT KENNEDY

Then - and only then – could I allow myself to experience any emotion. I found a quiet place on the island where I could be alone and for a few minutes I gave way to all my feelings, the despair, the hopelessness of the situation, the weight of responsibility, the loss of the crew members, everything I had been bottling up without realising it. It all came flooding out of me. When I reached a point of calm, I turned my thoughts to what I really needed to do at that moment, which was to give thanks to Almighty God that I and my crew members had survived. It could have been so much worse. 11 survived, 2 were lost. Considering the force with which PT109 was rammed, it was a living miracle that so many actually survived. I had much to be grateful for - and I was.

I need to go back to that traumatic, troublesome, controversial time for a moment, despite the fact I would prefer to move on. I said 'controversial' because despite being given a medal for my heroic actions, I was very aware of General MacArthur's comment that I should have been court-martialled rather than rewarded. It is very much a matter of opinion, his against those who considered I was worthy of being given a medal. Very briefly, I want to say that in many ways they are both wrong. The General, for all his experience, was not there when the incident occurred. I was following orders at the time when the boat was rammed, if I should not have been there then it was the result of a decision by the higher command; it was not of my doing. What I did was an instinctive reaction to save the lives of the men from the ship. I did not - and do not - consider myself a hero. So in reality I fell somewhere between the two, but I was not about to return the medal, it meant a lot at the time. (I apologise to the general for casting aspersions on his opinion, but am sure his shoulders are broad enough to take it.)

The truth was that the entire incident, with all that it entailed, including the loss of life, was a result of bad planning and management by those in command. That was part of the reason I did not believe I had earned the medal. I was attempting to undo something created through the inefficiency of others. That group should not have been there, in those waters, in that vessel, with a Japanese destroyer in the area. And that, dear readers, is a fact.

Physically it took me some time to get over that. As I said, my body and I were in constant battle with one another and that was another occasion when I felt it was letting me down.

I went back to the war zone. After a period of leave, in which I was able to recover, I went back, because I needed to fight. My self-esteem was at risk. And if you really want to know how I felt at that time, I confess to being full of anger. I could not get over the deaths of the two crew members, which was absolutely stupid considering the casualties incurred during the war, but this was personal.

I have decided against going further into my war experiences, they were and are a source of great discomfort and painful memories, a sense of not really being part of the ongoing war but having to take that which was given. Orders were orders, no matter what and sometimes it was not possible to circumvent them.

Some time later I was honourably discharged from the Marines. I had done my duty and went home with a chest full of medals. If anyone wants to read my war record, go look it up. I am not ashamed of it, but I am not proud of it. Had I been stronger in body I would have done much more. Yes, more than towing someone by fastening my teeth on the man's life-jacket! I saved lives and for those whose lives were saved that was critical, of course. But taken overall, the efforts I made were not much more than small punctuation mark in the great story that was the American involvement in the Second World War. I had no illusions about my time in uniform. I did my best but God alone knows how much I would have liked to have done much, much more.

Here I need to take time to think about the fact that the war claimed the life of my brother Joe. In my eyes he was a greater hero than I ever was, or ever would be. Joe flew mission after mission in heavy bombers and was entitled to come home, but decided to fly one more, the one that took his life. I wish the reader to remember that when they call me a war hero. I gave my all to rescue those with me; Joe gave his all in flying bombing raids which no doubt contributed to the ending of the war. No one can truly say how much a person contributed to anything in a war; everyone plays their part, no matter how big or small. Joe had been extremely cynical about my 'adventures', wanting to know how I managed to miss seeing a destroyer, but it was easy for him, he was not on board at the time.

I did not argue with Joe over it. What he was doing was far superior to any service I was giving, because as usual my body was winning the battle against my will to do things. I went on to have extensive surgery on my back. I had many 'internal' problems. I was given the last rites and it was a miracle to me that I lived as long as I did. The reader will recall I always said I would not make my 30th birthday. I really believed that was going to happen.

The family were grief-stricken at the news of Joe's death, whilst being proud that they had made a substantial contribution to the war effort. No one could say that the Kennedys, for all their wealth and influence, had held back from playing a meaningful part in the war. No one could deride them now they had made the supreme sacrifice, along with so many other families, the life of a much loved son.

I have found it extremely difficult to talk of my war years, of the loss of my brother, of the 'survivor guilt' which remained with me for a long time, with the great sadness my parents carried, for they never really came to terms with Joe's death so my own experiences are best left to the record books.

After all the surgery and physiotherapy and the painkillers, I emerged into a new life: politics.

Life Changing Days

John Fitzgerald Kennedy decides to take a new direction in life

I was 28 when I looked around at my life, thought about all I had been through, all that I had learned through experience, discussions with many different people, observations from travelling around part of the known world and of course the intense political discussions which had gone on endlessly in the family. I knew well that my brother Joe had been groomed to take office and I knew that by following that course I would be in part fulfilling my parents' dream. I had to ask myself what was the real basic reason I was seriously thinking of going into politics. Some people aspire to high office for no other reason than the standing it would give them in society. Some people aspire to it for the income that it would generate in the form of positions of power on this board or that. I often asked myself how many actually went into politics with a genuine desire to serve. That was what I needed to work out in my own mind, was I going into politics to serve, or to fulfil my family's ambitions, or simply because I needed to do something.

It was about this time I attended Mass which, usually, was something I went through by rote. Not on this occasion. I could not tell the reader what word or even words triggered the thought in my mind that I wished to serve the people of the USA. I knew that it reached back to thoughts I had in my youth, namely that I would do something - I did not know what – for my country. I mentioned that at the beginning of my book. But, I am talking many years from the time I made that vow to the person who was thinking of their future. I am also talking about extreme experiences during the intervening time, not only the colleges, but the travelling, the war itself, all that I went through during the problematic PT 109 debacle, which at that point of my life was the only way I could describe it. I often woke nights, re-living the nightmare of the five-hour swim, wondering how I had the strength to do it and sometimes I thought that that strength which I gained from somewhere to do that was identical to that which saw me through the surgery, the physiotherapy and the relentless pain my body had subjected me to. From all this I reasoned that the great power which ruled our lives, that which some call God and others refer to as spirit or any other designation, had some kind of plan for me, or else I too would have been a casualty of the war. Did that sound fanciful? If it did, put it down to the vagaries of the mind of someone who had suffered extraordinary experiences and who was then facing life decisions, any of which could take him in a direction which may not have pleased him.

It was as a result of this, which seemed like a shaft of light coming into a dark room, that I decided not to pursue a journalistic career but to apply myself to working toward taking political office.

Following this, my next decision was that I would do it on my own, that is, without any help from my father. I knew my father's reputation; I wanted no taint on my own political career. I am saying this without casting aspersions on my father; it would be unfair of me to do so. He made his own decisions, his own choices, if they were not ones I would have followed then that was my conscience speaking, not his. No one should judge another, especially when that other happens to be your father. I just knew that my father's way was not mine. I confess here that I used his influence to get into the Marines, but that subterfuge was necessary if I was to serve my country in the Armed Forces. I knew then that forging a bill of health -- how do I explain this without sounding contrary and hypocritical?

I feel I need to explore this for my readers.

Right, here goes.

The army refused to admit me because of my health problems. My conscience would not let me use the fact I had been 'rejected' by the army to avoid active service. I could not face spending the war years in a deskbound position. It was not in me to allow others to fight the battle against fascism for me. It mattered not that I was not physically capable of doing as much as the next man; I still felt I had to play my part. Because of this I used my father's and grandfather's influence first to get me into the Marines and then to get me into the front line. I had no idea that, as a result of this series of happenings, I would end up being called a war hero. As I said, to be a hero meant only that the person was in the right place at the right time and did not think through the consequences of any act that they did to help their fellow men.

Politics can be a dirty business. There is no doubt of that. I know many who had become rich through their political service, which they conducted without any true regard for their fellow countrymen. I had seen enough, experienced enough and was proud enough to want to be the kind of politician who genuinely worked for my fellow man, without putting myself first. I needed people to see that and to do that I had to fight the political battles on my own ground, albeit with the family name which I could not escape, but without the family influence. No one pulled the strings to get me my first office. I worked for it. When I discussed it with the family, I told them that was the way I wanted it. Here I need to say I knew my father tried to do some 'tinkering' to ensure I had a smooth ride but backed off, whilst busy pursuing his own political career. My father did so like being in the papers...

I thought the family went along with my decision to 'go it alone' to some degree, because they did not think I would ever attain high office. Nothing was said, but then who would say to someone aspiring to political life, 'you'll never make President, son.' Well, some might, but always hanging over everyone was the shadow of Joe. They did not attempt to dissuade me or pour cold water on higher ambitions. That was to have been Joe's career. That was to have been his life and they were watching the second son step into the first son's shoes. I had no illusions. I knew they would not fit me.

After a pause for thought, I decided to do something which would surprise my biographers. In one biography, it was clearly stated I had doubts about a political career, that it was not what I wanted and so on and so forth.

The book is totally wrong. It was very much what I wanted, but I decided not to rush into it and the best way to do that, to ensure there were no pressures, was to say' I'm not really sure yet. Give me time to make up my mind.' It was surprising how much space someone could gain for themselves in doing such a small thing, which really was nothing more than a mind game.

It was at this point I was beginning to put aside the shadow of my brother Joe, on the basis that Joe's life had finished and mine had a way to go. Despite my health problems, I felt I had something to offer to the USA and was determined to do it. And do it on my terms, not anyone else's. Some people thought I was lacking charisma that time; that I did not do the small talk, the political glad-handing well enough to make my mark on the world. They said I did not have the presence to go out and woo the voters and maybe, in many respects, they were right. But, determination can overcome all obstacles, including those of a supposed lack of charisma. The truth was I knew I could do it; all I needed was the incentive to get out there and tackle the job. So I made the decision to put Joe's shadow to one side. I decided I was definitely going to prove to the family once and for all that, second son or not, I was going to make it. And there was my personal private secret ambition: to walk into the White House as president.

I am now aware now of the school of thought which says if you think of something long enough, if you want it strongly enough, if you are prepared to fulfil the dream, you will make it. The theory is sound; it really does mean developing a mindset that gives you a dream and the determination not to let it go. No negativity is allowed to creep in and destroy the dream. That was what I did. I held the thought in my head; pictured myself standing on the lawn outside the White House speaking to the world, giving them my dream for the future of the USA. In this dream I had a beautiful woman at my side, the wife I had chosen and standing alongside her were the children. A dream, a dream to think of in the night when pain kept me awake, when the stomach decided to rebel and make life extremely uncomfortable, when pain killers were not killing the pain, then I thought of my dream and planned each detail of the speech I would make and even the suit I would wear. This was the first time the secret dream has been revealed, because this is the first time I have allowed myself to be truly honest about my feelings, ambitions and dreams for the career which I had decided on. It never was enough for me to change direction, to go into a new pathway and allow life to dictate what would happen to me. That was not my way. I wanted, if not actually needed, to dictate what happened in my life. That was a very different way of looking at things.

If the reader follows through my thinking in that previous paragraph, they will get an idea of the underlying driving force that pushed me into politics. The simple fact of making something happen. You cannot make something happen if you are a journalist, because you are reporting what has already happened.

As a writer you can perhaps change opinions, but it is a long, slow and tedious job. Equally, it must be remembered that not everyone will read the words you have laboured over and so your attempts to change something is very likely to be in vain. But in the Senate, ah, in the Senate you can be part of the decision-making process. How often did my memory return to the time when I sat in the Strangers' Gallery in the Houses of Parliament and listened to the debates about the war! I recalled very clearly the burning desire that swept through me, the desire to make my way down to the floor of the House and take part in the debate. There, you have another Kennedy secret exposed, something else which had been kept in the darkness of my mind for a good many years.

By now the reader should be getting a picture of someone who was slightly withdrawn, this mostly caused by fighting pain and the disability the pain bought with it, someone who knew exactly where they wanted to go but was busy hiding it to some degree so they would not be pressured into it, drawing on the secret desire to be part of the great decision-making going on in the world, rather than accepting other people's part in determining my life. I knew, without being told, that the supposed shyness or lack of confidence or whatever anyone wished to label it as, would disappear the moment I took the public stage. I remembered how it felt to read aloud at school and college, how it felt to join in debates, how it felt to argue politically sensitive points with anyone who was prepared to join in. All of this came together in a mind already full of experience, knowledge, determination and burning ambition. Looking back, I can see it was actually a winning combination. Looking back, it seems inevitable that I would end up anywhere but as President. But at the time... it was not that simple a prospect.

I knew how difficult it was going to be, I knew there would be an ongoing battle and whilst I had every confidence that I would win whatever seat I set out to capture, my underlying concern was – would my body stand up to the trials I would impose on it? Subsequent events would prove that at times my body did let me down, that I had to resort to using a wheelchair, but on the whole it was one battle which I did win. I got where I wanted to go. One of the 'advantages' of being assassinated was I was not voted out of office, as many are. I did not have to join the 'Ex-Presidents Club' which I believe I would have hated, without fully knowing why I think I would have hated it. I don't want to pursue that thought: it might lead into waters which are too muddy to navigate... What I will say is, once a president, always a president, because it is extremely difficult, if not impossible, to put aside the mind-set that comes with holding the most powerful position on earth. I know there would be some who will say that those who hold the equivalent position in Russia think they have the most powerful position and perhaps they do, in some regards. I don't think I want to argue this one, either!

What I am trying to do is give the reader a picture of how it felt to hold the ultimate position in the West. I was grateful that I did not have to pack up and leave the White House at the end of my tenure; I truly believe I would not have been able to handle that. So you see, for many reasons the assassination was a gift. A very strange gift, I agree, one which caused outrage, grief, heartache and consternation, because nothing was clear: even today the conspiracy theory continues to fascinate those who investigate such things.

But all this was very much in the future. Before then there are quite a few years to cover, some women to cover, some political goings-on and a lot more of my thoughts. In fact, it would not be inappropriate for me to apologise in advance for referring yet again to my assassination, which only had a place really at the end of the book when it terminated my 43 years. Unfortunately, it does tend to play a larger part than that in my life story insofar as it constantly comes into my thoughts. I trust that the reader will forgive me for this and I promise I will do my best to keep it low key if I can. I do not wish anyone to be bored. Somehow, I didn't think they will be.

Early Political Days

How John Fitzgerald Kennedy made his mark in the political arena

The first problem I had, one that was to plague me for a long, long time, was that Joe's shadow refused to go away. It was as if he walked alongside me, as if every political decision I took, Joe's hand was in it. In some interviews I actually said I would not be taking on the role if my brother was still alive. This was not entirely true, somewhere inside me I knew even if Joe had lived, if he was following the campaign trail, I would be elsewhere in the USA doing the same thing but seeking nomination for a different area. Politics was in my blood and I would not have been able to settle to a legal career after so much immersion in the political scene, at home, at college, during my war years and the time afterwards. I could not have sat in a lawyer's office and remembered that burning desire to go down on the floor of the House to take part in the debate and be content with my life. I had too much ambition for that. Oh yes there was a great opportunity for advancement in the law, maybe even reaching the Supreme Court, but it was not the same and I knew I would never turn my back on that secret, long held dream. In truth, I could not turn my back on that secret long held dream. To do that would have meant reneging on my conscience and my heart. I was not prepared to do that.

I was aware, despite my intentions that my father should not interfere with my political career, he was in fact arranging this and arranging that. It was as if, 'well, one son didn't live but the other is prepared to take on his role so I will do my best to smooth the way.' It was not what I wanted. But how do you argue with the man who had influenced your entire life?

My health became problematic at this time; the mirror showed a gaunt, haunted figure, suffering goodness knows what. I don't want to relate all the illnesses, symptoms, tests, for it would become as utterly boring to the reader as it was to me. I hated being ill. I never came to terms with it, the way some people do and accept that they are no more than a walking pincushion for doctors. I could not do that. I foresaw years of being pushed, prodded and poked and dreaded it. All things taken into consideration, perhaps I should have become a lawyer. At least then I would have been able to sit behind a desk and not subject myself to endless rallies, standing for hours, making speech after speech, attempting to bring people round to my way of thinking. But if you make a decision, you need to stand by it. In my heart of hearts I had committed myself to the political arena to help the people of the United States and that was what I intended to do.

If I stop and think about that period of time, the question which arises is this: if the bullet had not found me, would the illness have struck me down instead? There I go again, bringing the assassination back into the story...

My first attempts at being a political commentator -- representative -- call me what you wish, was not entirely successful. I wasn't good at small talk; it seemed to grate on me. I thought in part this was because it was to some degree false and I did not like it. I could not pretend to laugh; I could not easily bring myself to make foolish jokes or snappy off-the-cuff comments. I would write my speeches and stick with them. I quickly realised that what went down in college would not go down well with voters. I had to do a rethink and there I have to confess my father did help me. Together we analysed the speeches and worked on them, aiming to make the next one better and so on and so I improved.

No, not improved -- gained in confidence. I always knew what I wanted to say, I always knew how I wanted to put it across, but the audiences were bigger than I was used to. Sometimes they were hostile and I needed the ability to cope with the feelings coming at me from the audience. Every speech I made took me a tiny step nearer to gaining the confidence of the electorate which I so desperately needed. I already believed in myself, I had to believe in what I could do. The two things were quite different. Politics, unfortunately, is as much a game as anything. You learned to play the game, or get left on the side-lines.

Nothing has been said but I am aware I have reverted to telling the reader the facts rather than telling them how I felt. My problem is, even after all this time, I am used to explaining the facts, concealing how I felt. It was not a good thing to show emotion in public, unless it was appropriate for the occasion. By this I mean it was right to look solemn at events commemorating the war dead or the death of a prominent citizen, to smile and be happy on festive occasions, but my own inner feelings had to be concealed. Only my close family knew of my despair at times, my need to bring policies to the people which were right for them, in my eyes, at least.

In an effort to rectify that, I want to tell my reader that at times I felt fear, the ancient fear of losing, the fear of rejection, the fear that my dream would be shattered before it became reality. I felt inadequate in social gatherings, wondering how I could develop the persona everyone seemed to want from me. I felt awkward and almost embarrassed when my father pointed out the obvious errors in my speeches, but I learned and, in learning, the fear began to recede, along with the nerves that plagued me at times. I was taken aback at the antagonism from the start, not having taken that into consideration when making my plans. And no one had thought to forewarn me about it, either, not that it would have made much difference to the way I felt.

It seemed the moment I declared my intention to enter the political race, the antagonism started. On reflection I thought it was just as well it began immediately. I needed to learn how to battle this because I would go on battling it for the rest of my natural life. Everyone who enters the political arena, or anything that brings you before the public, immediately brings critics from the woodwork. Any singer, musician, group, film star, television personality or author, no matter in what they might excel, will attract not only criticism but possibly derision, too. Most writers suffer rejection when they begin their career, so they are used to their work being criticised, for others it is often a good deal more difficult. I found it especially difficult at first, because I had the wonderful feeling that I was on a crusade to do good for the American people. To walk into opposition before I had even begun rather took me aback but as I said, it was just as well because it gave me an insight as to what future political life would be like. I did not expect to be loved by all, no one is, no matter how good they are, what their intentions are; what message of peace or otherwise they bring to the world, they are not universally loved or even liked. It came as part of the job.

Having said that, antagonism was, by its nature, hurtful. Accepting it wasn't easy. But then when did anything good ever come easy? I knew I had work to do to become accepted by the electorate and was prepared to do it. Fortunately, my experiences in the Marines were widely enough known for the 'war hero' tag to be put on me. I also came with a different background, that made me someone apart, not your run-of-the-mill politician. There were those who backed me and there were more of them than those who tried to denigrate me and so, with all the luck that my family connections, the name, my war record and everything else that could be thrown into the melting pot could give him, John Fitzgerald Kennedy launched his new career. It had a 50-50 chance of succeeding. If it failed, at least I could say I tried. If it succeeded, there was only one way to go -- to the very top. In my heart I knew that was where I was going to go.

I was moving into a time of tremendous upheaval in my life. I had to do things which at first were alien to me, like going into bars and other places, stand on street corners, with people, finding out their needs, their aspirations, their dreams, to understand what the people of the United States really wanted from their leaders.

I was out early to talk to factory workers, I really did knock on doors and talk to people. I went wherever they were and found within myself a great need to do this, quite apart from and separate from the need to get votes. As far as the world was concerned I was canvassing for votes. As far as I was concerned I was studying the heart of the American people. These were two very different things. It took its toll, of course, I was not the fittest of people before it began and very soon I became a bit of a wreck (my diagnosis) but it worked. There was something in what I was saying, or doing, or both, which was striking chords with the people. That was what mattered. What I learned then stood me in very good stead for the rest of my political life. No one could say I did not understand grassroots people and grassroots needs. Political opponents will jump on anything to bring someone down, that was one thing they could not throw at me.

The only thing they could throw at me was the amount of money my father spent on my campaign. But you see, I thought; if you have money, you use it. Others had to draw money from supporters. I didn't. What this did in turn was give me even more work.

There I was, the rich man's son, with those who would never see such wealth, working to convince them that I understood where their dreams and hopes and ambitions actually lie. It was just another burden for me to carry. If you like, another mountain for me to climb, along with being a candidate with a bad back and other physical limitations!

There were many events in my campaign, all written out for the reader if they want to go and find them, but the upshot of it all was that I was elected and that was all that mattered at the time.

I began this section talking about my brother's shadow, which haunted me for a long time. I have to confess that when I won a major victory and took my place in my country's political system, my brother's shadow shrank to something around the size of my footprint. It, and he, never entirely went away, nor would I expect him to. But the family accepted me as the first son, the one who was going to make my mark, the one who finally came good. It was enough for me.

Married Life

How John Fitzgerald Kennedy became a family man

It was time, in every way, to forget the girls and think about marriage. That sounds remarkably like a political decision on my part, but it wasn't. The decision was made the moment I was introduced to Jacqueline Lee Bouvier. If there was anyone else at that dinner party I disremember who they were and if there were other women in my life at that time I disremember who they were, too. My eyes, my heart, my mind, was full of Jacqueline - no one else existed. Now, if only that state of affairs -- the word was chosen carefully -- had continued throughout our marriage...

Well, for one thing I would not need to write this book. Now, that may or may not have been a good thing. For me, egotistical still as I am, that would have been a bad thing, because I would have approached the channel and said: 'would you write my story for me?' knowing there was nothing in particular that needed to be revealed. I would have been doing it for my own ego. I am sure you would have welcomed the book anyway, says me with the utmost conceit, but the fact is this, there are many authors waiting to come to talk about momentous events in their lives, some because they are misunderstood, some because they are maligned and others, like myself, who have something on their conscience which they must clear if they are to find peace. What I am saying is; it would have been unfair of me to come if I had not had something momentous to tell the world. So, because of the womanising, yes, there is something to tell.

But I have to return to the point at which I was before I diverted. I met Jacqueline and fell in love. She was everything I wanted in a partner and wife, she had the breeding, the background, the family, the looks, need I go on? There were many times I asked myself why she married me, what she saw in me to make her forsake others, those who would have been possibly better suited, ones who would not have cheated on her and ultimately left her a widow at an early age. I could only assume her love for me was as big as my love for her and for that I was - and am - eternally grateful.

As far as everything else was concerned, my problem was, quite simply, I had it all but I wanted more.

On that admission I closed the work session. I did not realise I was going to reveal quite so much, did not realise just how deep I was digging, so the revelation rather shocked me. I thought about having it deleted, but no -- this book is the truth and that statement is the truth.

But going back to Jacqueline, for me it was more like finding a soul-mate than a wife. It was as if she knew my every mood, thought, even the words before they left my mouth. At first it was disconcerting, then I realised it was the greatest asset I could have, a partner who would stand by me through all the turmoil of canvassing, campaigning, socialising and generally working flat-out to convince the voters I was the man they wanted. This went on long after I had been elected, for no one could turn their back on the electorate and expect them to go on supporting them. The one thing people have to realise is that when someone puts a foot on the political pathway, it is very hard to step off of it again. People tend to think 'campaigning' all their waking hours, looking for opportunities to talk with people, to make an impression, seeking out that next interview, the next broadcast, the next scheduled appearance, the next unscheduled appearance. Reporters and journalists track their every move, writing it up for the papers from their perspective which often differs considerably from their own. It takes an exceptional woman to stand by her husband in this kind of environment. My wife did it superbly. At no time could anyone fault her, could not pick her words to pieces and accuse her of bias. She was a diplomat to her very bones. I was not ashamed to admit she taught me a great deal, how to handle just about any situation that presented itself, how to talk to people, how to simply be. It was as if her breeding, her upbringing, rubbed off on me to the point when it was natural, so that I did not have to give it a single thought.

Jacqueline taught me the greater art of small talk, how to mix gracefully at cocktail parties, what to wear and how to wear it. Small, almost insignificant things but they built up slowly so it became part of my persona. And I fell more deeply in love with her every day.

Our wedding was a big Society affair, with everyone who was anyone in attendance. The handsome bachelor marrying the beautiful Jacqueline. I could not have asked for a greater amount of publicity for us both. And I could not have been happier, either.

The reader would be entitled to ask why, with such a perfect wife, I should have been playing the field with others. The answer is both simple and complex. Simple in that my vanity was at the root of it. I needed to know at all times that I was desirable, able to attract women, able to satiate the overwhelming sex drive which I seemed incapable of curbing and to impress those who were in my circle of friends and acquaintances. They were, quite frankly, envious, which added to my ego and made me feel good. So there was a vicious circle. I needed the women to make me look good in the eyes of others which in turn made me feel good and at the same time satiated my sex drive. With that kind of circle, it was not a question of my inability to break it but that I did not want to break it. I knew of course that money talked with many women and even more than that, when I became president the power talked, too. It was then that my need for women grew even stronger because I still needed to prove to myself it was me they wanted, not the money or what my position could bring them. The reader will appreciate this was a somewhat twisted scenario and I do not even know now if I have rationalised it fully to myself or the world. I can only say I have done my best to explain it. People do not always fully understand their own motives, or the agendas that they set themselves without realising it. They were not always given clear insights into themselves. By the time anyone reads this, I would have been 'dead' for over 50 years, a period I spent thinking about my life and wondering what would have happened if I had taken this course or that instead.

For example, if I had not pushed to go into the Marines, not become a war hero, gone into law rather than politics, would I have been happier? I would have been considerably healthier. From Day One campaigning took an immense toll on my body, but should anyone trade a relatively mundane life for a more comfortable one? Some would argue it was the best thing to do, mollycoddle the body at the cost of ambition and drive. I can understand that point of view. Indeed, there were times when I heartily wished I did not have to go out and shake hands and talk and stand and be cold, when there was an overwhelming longing to do no more than lie down in a warm bed, close my eyes and allow sleep to take over. Having said that, I knew from thinking about my life that I would have stagnated very fast in that kind of environment. I would have been frustrated and probably utterly bored. This would not have been good for me at all. With relatively little to occupy my mind, the conditions from which I suffered would have exaggerated themselves to the point when health would have become of primary importance and I would have been the most terrible bore on the subject. As it was, I had so much to occupy my mind, everything from family to the electorate, campaigns to be planned, endless meetings to attend, speeches to give, that bad health was pushed into the background and there it stayed. When forced into hospital for surgery, I battled every moment of every day to get well because there was much to do. Being given the last rites only fuelled my determination to get out of bed and start work again.

Foolish? I didn't think so. It is very easy to fall into the trap of feeling sorry for yourself, to complain all the time about this pain and that, to the point when people stop asking you how you are. I would not have that. I held firm to the vow I made to myself, that my body would not win the battle - nor did it. I am extremely proud of that.

I have come some distance from talking about my wife, but that seems to be the nature of this book. I begin with a topic and it leads me in other directions, all of which, I trust, are revealing aspects of myself to the reader.

For a moment I wished to revert to my early days, when I was little more than a struggling politician with a beautiful wife, campaigning non-stop, trying to throw off the background with which I was tainted at the time, trying to establish myself as a credible person in the eyes of my fellow Americans. My memory of those times is of forcing myself to do things which were beyond what I would normally have done, but which were extremely good for me having done it. I never forgot, no matter what power or wealth I had, that the vast majority of my fellow Americans did not have the same privileges as I did. I was very aware it was not possible for all of them to achieve the same status I had. There could only be one leader, the rest must follow, but if there was a way to improve their standard of living, then I would try and find it. If there was a way of increasing their security from outside forces, then I would find a way to do it. Everyone's needs, ambitions, security, wealth, came from being strong, never from being weak. The USA needed strong leaders; I was determined to be one of them.

Whether I succeeded is for history to determine. I did the best I could with the situation at the time, those I had to work with me and the political climate in the world then. No one works or lives in isolation. It is only when I held the supreme position of power that I realised the full truth of John Donne's oft quoted words, 'no man is an island.' Leaving aside the rest of it, think on those words and what they mean. Everyone likes to think they are individuals, believing they can live their lives without reference to anyone else, indulge their every whim, literally do as they please. They cannot. Whatever anyone does affects others, sometimes in a big way, sometimes in a small way, but it always has an effect. Imagine the dominoes falling, the slightest lightest touch on the first of many dominoes stood on end will send them all tumbling. I held the domino image in my mind many times. It was a good one to think on. When a leader is about to make a decision that will affect millions of people, it was a good moment to reflect on the Domino Effect, something to be borne in mind before signing the papers committing the country to a particular piece of legislation. That especially had merit when it was associated with the defence budget, the space race, taxation, or the possibility of war. Despite all the USA had suffered in the way of war casualties, there were still high-ranking officers who were prepared to take the country into more conflict. They came close, did they not, at several times, occasions when I felt I was walking a tightrope that would either plunge the USA into conflict or enhance its standing in the world. There was very little space between those two things. My reputation was very much on the line, but that was something every politician had to deal with and learn to live with. They say writers need to grow a thick skin; I say politicians do as well.

I have come a very long way from the heading I put on this section, of how I became a family man. The problem is, no matter what I do or say in this book, I have to confess that political life intruded on every single thing I did.

The one thing I didn't want to do -- but have to -- is talk about the children. The miscarriage, the stillbirth, the loss of our son Patrick, all were devastating. People are going to say, that goes without saying and I would agree with them. But think on this, the devastation it caused myself and my wife went very deep because we became the First Family and as such were representative of family life in the USA. That life did not seem to be happening ... because of these deaths.

But we had our beautiful Caroline and our handsome John and we cherished them. Life at the White House with them was wonderful. But there again I am getting ahead of myself. I would only say this is what transpired later. Before then there was just Jacqueline and myself and the driving ambition to get to the White House. It wasn't easy.

Campaigning Days

How John Fitzgerald Kennedy ended up in the White House

When someone decides to run for office, they take the first step on a very long, convoluted, rocky pathway. It has many potholes, rocks, diversions, an infinite amount of *no entry* signs and a great many *exit* signs put there by political commentators, other senators, opponents, enemies and sometimes even friends. Nothing is given to them, they earn every good word, every vote, every accolade, they all go together to make the leaves that finally come together in the victor's laurel wreath. At least, that was the way I saw it.

I had a problem during the campaigning; a major one. I did not cast a vote one way or the other in the decision to censure Joseph McCarthy. The truth is - I could not decide which way to vote. Did I go with my conscience, or did I go with friendship? It is almost impossible to tell the reader the trauma I went through turning this over in my mind, first one way and then the other. Whatever decision I made would be damaging, the only alternative was to make no decision at all. That brought its own problems, but they were not as difficult to cope with as the consequences of voting would have been. Did I turn against a family friend, or did I support that family friend? It seemed that many were waiting for me to decide, but I was in hospital where I was heavily doped on morphine. I stared at the hospital ceiling and there wrote (metaphorically) my reasons for versus my reasons against and then on the third column I wrote the consequences of abstaining. In the end that was the route I took. Although it did damage, it also saved me from what I felt would have been a bad decision. I know Eleanor Roosevelt didn't understand this and I also know she would not have understood had I explained it to her. Some people tend to see the world in such sharp contrast of black and white that to offer them a shade of grey is beyond their comprehension.

It was just one of the problems I ran into during my campaigning. The other problem was the toll it took on my health. I had to say though there was nothing like fighting pain to keep the mind firmly on what is being discussed, whether it be with someone on the street, someone on the television, some political journalist trying their very best to catch the person out, or those of my own party who would play devil's advocate with questions, preparation for anything thrown at me whilst out there among the people. It worked. Both ways it worked. Those in my campaign headquarters worked tirelessly for me; in turn I pushed my body to its limit to work tirelessly for them. When so many people commit themselves to the cause, it is incumbent on the candidate to do more than their fair share in return.

Something else I had to fight during my campaigning was the loss of my sister. Apart from the great hole it left in my life, it added to my sense of mortality. The more I work on the book, the more I realise how appropriate the title is. I not only walked with Joe's shadow at my heels, I also had Death walking there too. Even now, looking back over my life, I still believe some deaths were senseless, serving no real purpose and others, whilst heartbreaking, at least made a small contribution to the greater whole. In the midst of grief it is not easy to see any reason why anyone dies before their time. For myself, constantly battling my own conditions, I was grateful for every day I lived, whatever that day be loaded with: sorrow, tiredness, pain, aggravation and at times a sense of hopelessness, for the task was huge and the country even bigger. I would often go to bed thinking I would be spending the rest of my life on the road, campaigning without an end - a living nightmare. And yet, I was determined to ensure that during the days I did live, I made a contribution in some way or other. It may have been nothing more than a word in the right place, a potential voter having a point of policy clarified, a co-worker complimented and their confidence renewed, or a problem lifted; you name it, I tried to do it. It was as if I was under some kind of compulsion to do more and more and more, even when people were telling me I had done enough. I thought at that time it was I who would say when I had done enough, not they.

What I don't want to do is to give the reader a day by day, week by week, account of my campaigning. They don't need to know, in this book, what the policies were, the stance I took, what I said about Republicans and so on. It is all written already. Everything I said, everything I did, is documented. In this modern age of information, everything is logged all the time and if the reader really wants to know, there are sufficient books on my life for them to find all they want to read. My concern with this book is to give the reader the inner Jack Kennedy, the one who sometimes looked out at the campaigning and the politicking and the shenanigans of others who were trying to steal my votes and I would smile. I had already said I did not have the ability to foresee anything, other than that which I desired, but something told me that I would achieve every office I set out to gain, no matter the cost. A dream that becomes an obsession has to be fulfilled or the person is left unsatisfied for the rest of their lives. I knew I walked in Death's shadow, so I was determined I would indeed achieve my aims so that the life I had before me, which I knew would not be long, would not be wasted in regretting unfulfilled dreams.

To fulfil my dreams I used the family wealth. It was not what I really wanted at the time, but having infinite wealth available and the ability to tap into it to make my dream come true it made it something I had to do. Sometimes you have to go with what is there, I said.

Maybe I overwhelmed my opponents with what I was able to spend, if so that was my fortune – no pun intended – and I would have been foolish to have ignored it. I would ask any one of you reading this book - would you turn your back on the chance to use a fantastic amount of money to gain what you wanted: a step on the political ladder? When you have an obsessive dream, you take and do everything that is there to help you realise that dream.

So you saw my name on billboards, on leaflets, on posters for speeches, the opportunities to meet and speak on political matters and then having achieved the first part of the dream, to see my name in newspapers and on television... there really was no end to the publicity drive to put a Kennedy where I wanted to be -- in front of everyone's eyes so that they would not forget me when the time came to vote.

And so, step-by-step I worked my way up the political ladder. The only thing that was missing from my life was a partner, one I could trust, when I could lean on, someone who understood me.

And I found her at a cocktail party, radiant, beautiful, charming – and mine. As I had already said, she became everything to me: soul mate, confidant, friend, lover, campaign partner and later, mother of my much-loved children.

In many ways our wedding and lifestyle was a continuation of my constantly being in the limelight, but for her it seemed a little more difficult. The media intrusion seemed to disconcert her quite a bit. It was something she grew into, becoming the perfect companion for someone with such soaring political ambitions, but it was not easy for her.

And so the Kennedys settled down to married life. I would be the first to admit that marriage was not all roses, for there were two other great influences on my life and in my life which constantly got in the way.

115

When a relationship, or marriage, is new, it needs nurturing. Unfortunately, I had my feet firmly on the political ladder and that, more than anything, took priority. I would spend time with my campaign team, with my speech writers, studying, working out how to approach the next problem, how to win over a few more voters, anything to keep me on the upward path to my ultimate goal. I also could not relinquish the chase of pretty women. No matter my intention to remain faithful, the sensual side of me would not permit this and on many occasions I managed to leave my wife alone while I went off with someone else. I know she found this extremely difficult to cope with; it is something I regret bitterly even now, but admit my addiction to sex got in the way all the time. The more well-known I became, the harder it became to fend off the approaches of women attracted by my presence and in truth I was not really strong enough to keep them at arm's length. If there was a half a chance of bedding them, I would do so.

There was one occasion which I find causes me great shame and embarrassment even now, after all these years. To play around when your wife is pregnant is bad enough, not to return to her when the pregnancy ends in miscarriage is unchivalrous in the extreme. I am aware that is a bad word, if not a word that doesn't actually exist, but I am also aware that I can find nothing else which properly conveys what I felt - and feel - about that time. I was so caught up in my own world that I was not able to give a thought to hers. That seems extreme, the fact I am prepared to say that I was not able to give a thought to her world, but I insist that it is the truth. When I was with my wife she was everything to me, when I was away from her, pretty women would always catch my eye and draw my attention.

I admit to having had a compartmentalised mind, everything in its own convenient box. Family stayed in one box, politics in another, sexual escapades and dalliances in a third. This was the only way I could cope because family brought its own pressures, with my parents advising me to do this or that, whilst knowing that my father carried on exactly the same dalliances as I did. Politically I had to give everything to the campaign, to the office I had already gained; to every step I needed to take to fulfil my own personal dream and sometimes that meant excluding everything and everyone else. I then created a fourth box into which I put my wife. Later I would put my children into the same box with her and there I believed they would be safe. Looking at it from a distance, I realise that whilst I had four separate boxes in my mind, others did not. She surely wished to eliminate the box containing the other women, she would no doubt have liked a greater role in the political part of my life and certainly my family would have liked to have seen a good deal more of me. I was incapable of seeing at the time that the boxes should not have existed, everything should have had its own place interlocked with everything else. The problem is; it was not something I could do. From an early age I had created boxes and there they were. It was as if by moving from one box to the other, I could shut the other one away and pretend it did not exist. What I overlooked was the simple fact that others did not see the boxes, they saw me as a whole; they saw me as a womanising person with soaring ambitions, someone who at times had to be held back from doing something which would have jeopardised my ambitions. I was and am eternally grateful to the farseeing friends who warned me about some of the more serious things I was doing which would have stopped me going any further politically. I am relieved now I had the sense to listen to them. At the time I resented their interference and their 'rightness' in the situations. It's always difficult to accept you're wrong.

Quite apart from the problems within the marriage, my health began to fail me quite considerably at this time and I had to make decisions about surgery. I do not wish to detail the many medical problems and procedures I had to endure, for even now they are a memory I could well do without. They were invasive, intrusive, painful and most of all debilitating. For someone who wished to be up and about and doing, to be getting on with their life, it was all extremely difficult to cope with. I knew, though, that I could not go on with such incredible back pain, stomach condition, crippling headaches and everything else that bothered and tasked me. Something had to go.

And so I committed myself to surgery, which partially resolved the problems. I despaired at times of ever achieving my goal, my ambition, but something very deep inside determined to keep me going. Despite being close to death's door and even at times feeling as if the last rites were helping me through that door, I hung on to life, determined as I said to keep going. I held the picture in my head of walking out into the Rose Garden of the White House and surveying what would literally be my domain. That kind of image, if you hold onto it hard enough, can get you through the worst of times and these were the worst of times. New wife, new family and extensive back problems that I could have done without. The rest of me reacted badly too, the ongoing drugs did not help my stomach at all. What it did to me emotionally was another matter entirely, it took all my willpower to keep focused on that dream, but that was where the determination came in. It would have been so easy to have given up, to have settled for that sedentary life, the one I gave up to go into politics. But that was not my way, never had been. Each time my feet touched the hospital floor, it gave me an incentive to use those feet to walk out of the hospital and resume my life. And I did. It meant convalescence, it meant time away from the Senate, but the operations did help, much as I resented them.

Fortunately for me, I was seen as a brave and courageous man to go through that, rather than somebody who was weak, disabled and consequently ineffectual, which is what I did not want. The decisions did not come easy. Not only decisions on my health, but the decision I made on the McCarthy problem haunted me, I felt I should have handled it differently. Hindsight is always 20/20 vision. However, whatever I did I had to live with it. Sometimes, I thought, life could be extremely difficult.

This is a good moment to confirm that my book *Profiles In Courage* was indeed co-authored by Ted Sorensen. I would ever be grateful for his contribution. I also acknowledge him as a fine speech writer. He was essential if not integral to my campaigning. I want to say, you are not forgotten, Ted. Well, I had to do something whilst convalescing so I thought, why not do another book?

Politically, life was up and down, there were battles with others, some of them very unpleasant, which I had to learn to cope with. No matter how irate, angry or frustrated I got, I had to find a way round it, come at the problem from the different angle, to ensure that my opponents never had the last word. I was able to do it every time, which I was grateful for as it gave me considerable experience which I would need later.

Presidential Aspirations
John Fitzgerald Kennedy enters the arena...

During Christmas 1956, after consultations with my family and campaign staff, the decision was made for me to run for the presidency. I was in reasonable health at that time, capable of taking on the campaign burden, feeling confident in myself as a person, a critical component in a political career. It seemed like a good time to make my move toward establishing the reality of my dream.

I looked at the sentences I have just written and realised that once again I am sliding back into facts, which I had decided not to do. It is perfect for a biography; it is not perfect for someone who is giving their feelings to the reader. I also realise that the paragraph above it was also based on facts and not on feelings and know I have to rectify this.

A political life is never a smooth one. There are enemies without and within, there are people who take a total opposite stand to you and fight their corner vociferously. Sometimes there is mud-slinging, sometimes there is a good deal of serious insulting, sometimes it was extremely difficult to defend yourself against allegations without resorting to the same tactics. It was times like these I needed the companionship of my wife, who was a calming steady influence on me and my campaign team whom I trusted completely. My father was a great influence as well, having been there and suffered the same slings and arrows as I did. Somebody who had endured and survived the political arena, as Joe Kennedy had was invaluable to someone fighting their own battles at this time. And so the Kennedys, together, set out to conquer the USA. Step by step, article by article, battle by battle, taking up this cause and that, getting my name out everywhere and proving I was fighting for the people, not for myself and gathering support as I went. Sometimes it felt good, sometimes I despaired, but all the time I knew I would not exchange the life for any other. It mattered little that my health was at risk, because I felt I had achieved my aim and become a consummate politician. It was with all this background that the decision was made to run for the presidency.

I know it is not enough just to say that, I know my readers will want more. A decision that large needs a good deal of consideration, weighing up the pros and cons. The cost, literally and physically, deprivation, being away from home for great lengths of time whilst campaigning, emotionally, having to be on show with nothing private from the intrusive commentators and journalists, as well as battling the enemies within and without, was immense. It took many discussions with family, the campaign team, sympathetic friends and advisors, before it was finally decided yes, we would go for it.

And in making that decision, I felt as if a huge weight had been taken from me which, looking at it dispassionately was stupid, looking at it emotionally was right. The dream was within my grasp. I had come so far; I only had to make one more supreme effort. The 'weight' had been the fear that I would not be able to even think about making that one last effort, if my health broke down, if my family was against it, if my campaign team did not think I was capable of doing it – there were a hundred things which could have gone against me - but didn't.

It was almost there.

As with everything concerned with politics, though, it was fraught with difficulties. My Catholicism seemed to be against me in many places. Even though I expected it in the more Protestant areas, it tended to be an issue in other locations, too. It was a difficulty I had foreseen but handling it needed diplomacy which varied from place to place. It was another experience, one I needed to help me further along the Presidential route. All experience is good, I told myself, after yet another 'battle' with yet another commentator.

Unfortunately, a lot of ill health dogged my political ambitions. I spent many miserable lonely days in hospital, being treated for all sorts of conditions, from my back pain to the crippling colitis. It is fair to say it was only my intense desire, coupled with burning ambition to make it to the top, which drove me on. I would not have been criticised by anyone had I withdrawn from the race but I would not have been able to live with myself if I did. All the travelling, the campaigning, the speech making, all the ground work I had done aiming for the Vice Presidency, despite my failure to achieve it, would be undone, wasted, thrown into the murky depths of history if I abandoned the task. That was not my way.

There was also the question of the shadow of Joe. Small though it was, it still dogged my every footstep. For Joe's sake I had to go on, to fulfil that which Joe would have done had he lived, to fulfil the family's dream of at least one person holding the supreme office. With that kind of motivation, there was no way I could not go on.

I have been standing back from my book for some time, considering the statements I have made. Were they pure facts which would bore, or were they from my heart, in which case they should carry the ring of truth?

It was not an easy time. Health problems, which relented to let me go out campaigning and then flared up again to take me out of the political arena, secretly, for fear of it damaging my work, were one major concern. The impact on my family life was another. My ever-conscious thought of my brother was a third. Over it all hung the biggest thing of all – KENNEDY – the family, the clan. The pride of my father, the approbation of the rest of them was something I sought without being able to rationalise fully why, unless the simple thought of being 'second son' still lingered. It should have been dismissed long before; it should have been cast away with the garbage. It wasn't. It hadn't. It was a constant presence and one I resented and yet knew I had to accept. I was a Kennedy; part of the clan. Whatever I did reflected on the rest. I also wanted to fulfil my brother's dream for him. It was difficult to admit this, but I felt a bounden duty to gain the presidency for my brother. I knew if I made it -- change that to when I made it -- the first thing I would do would be to give thanks to God I had achieved it and the second thing would be to dedicate the position and power to Joe. Only when I had made that statement would I feel free to carry on with my life. Up to and including that moment there were two Kennedys walking toward the White House. The problem was, only I knew it. It would not do to tell anyone anyway, they would not understand and even if they had a glimmer of understanding, they would not appreciate the shadow Joe had cast over my life virtually from day one. Death had not removed Joe; it had merely moved him on to the sidelines where he cheered his brother on endlessly, enthusiastically, without the merest hint of jealousy. But then, when did a bomber pilot who had given his life for his country ever had need to be jealous of a younger brother who was sick, virtually disabled and whose war record only held heroism by the merest chance of him being in the right place at the right time with the right level of determination to save his men?

It was at that point that I was again confronted with the memory of my war record and again say I did not deserve the accolade of war hero, did not deserve the medals, did not deserve the coverage PT 109 engendered, but -- reluctantly --I accept it played a very big part in my campaign. It was an essential ingredient of my standing as a candidate and, more than that, what had been done could not be undone in the eyes of the public. Once acknowledged as a war hero, unless you are found to be fraudulent in that heroism, it stays with you forever. And so, with all those reservations, I decided if I had to be a war hero, I would be one. If it helped the campaign, then I would go with it. But in my heart I knew I would never equal Joe's amazing contribution. In my quiet moments I would tell my brother this and listen for the laughter I knew so well. In some of my lighter moments I thought I actually heard it.

The Pulitzer Prize for *Profiles In Courage* did a lot to help the campaign and the publicity which went with it was worth a fortune to the Kennedys. Good and bad, that is, for all publicity helps, no matter what it is. Someone claims there is fraud over the sales figures? Let the papers run with that, everyone decided, because the more they discussed it, the more the book and the author were mentioned. Nothing bad about that, especially as nothing was proved. Because, it was not there to be proved! The sales were genuine. It was just that some people didn't want to believe it.

But then, success is usually resented by someone somewhere and when that 'someone' happens to be a group of people who did not want the Kennedys to make headway in the political world, they sought any ammunition and any weapon to try and stop them. It did not seem to occur to them that the good of the people should come before any personal animosity toward anyone attempting to gain office, no matter at what level. Unfortunately, that was – and is - the way of politics. So many people venture into the political arena for their own ends, for their own agenda, not for good of the country as a whole. I have a distinct feeling I have said this already. I do not want to waste time checking it, because I felt it does not matter. It is something I feel

very strongly about and repetition would not come
amiss.

Facing Up To Reality

The moment JFK realises the world is not his for the taking after all

After all the work, all the effort, all the illness, all the family upheavals, the campaign failed. It was obviously not my time, the mood of the country, mood of the people, even the mood of the party had to be right for me to make that final breakthrough.

The breakthrough came but it took another four years.

As has happened several times during the writing of this book, I had to stand back, look at what I had written and realise that once again it was nothing more than facts. The problem is, I freely admit, it is easier to hide behind facts then delve for true feelings and put them onto paper. If I've said this already, then accept it really is a fact I need to rectify or the book will fail, just as the campaign did.

The truth is; I was bitterly disappointed at the failure. I looked to blame myself a good deal rather than look at the overall picture, but there was little I could do about it. It was not my time. That was difficult to accept when you have nurtured a dream for a long time, when the dream has been something to hold onto throughout all the long periods of convalescence, when it has been the mainstay of the family. To have to admit failure was exceedingly hard to do. There were many reasons for the failure, all have been dissected many times, in many books, pulled apart by many political journalists and I have no intention of recycling the arguments in this one. It is enough to say that I had a further four years to wait for my time to come, with the added disadvantage of not really knowing whether that time would come, or whether I would have to wait all over again. It was not a good time, but in many ways it was necessary. I had the opportunity to broaden my political experience, of being on committees, of doing more canvassing, of being able to assess more closely the mood of the people, but all of this only became apparent when I launched into my new campaign for the presidency. At that point I knew I had been fortunate in not being voted in four years earlier. If only I had seen it at the time of the disappointment of losing, it would have been much easier to take.

In the great master plan which controls all our lives, there are ebbs and flows of time, peaks and troughs, of fortunes and misfortunes, all of which are designed to take us to the point when the flows and peaks and fortunes come together. Where I had previously been fighting for opportunities to put my point across, by 1957 I was speaking in states right across the continent and by 1958 the demands for me to speak were so great I could not possibly fulfil them all. By this time the much-loved President Eisenhower was visibly weakening and my youth, energy and apparent zest for life was a startling contrast. I attracted attention everywhere I went, which pleased me very much. This time everything went right, and I was nominated as the presidential candidate by the Democratic Party virtually by default. Not that it was an easy ride, there were those who would have preferred me to try for the vice presidency on the grounds of my youth and others who would prefer me not to stand because I was a Catholic. I had no time for anyone who tried to push me into being second. If I could not be first I did not want to know. I also did not believe my Catholicism should have got in the way, I believed in religious freedom along with political freedom, something I fought for in every way I could.

I was exhilarated by being nominated, but had to put it to one side and concentrate, the task ahead was huge. I leaned heavily on Jackie throughout this time, she was my support, my confidant, in many ways my rock.

Electioneering is extraordinarily demanding. Everyone concerned has to be totally committed, family life has to be put to one side, someone has to remind you about birthdays and anniversaries and other such important occasions, because the speaking, the travelling and making yourself known on a personal level to the country as vast as the United States is something beyond description. You do it, you commit yourself to it, you take the trains or the cars and attend the speaking engagements and the parties, the receptions, the endless round of being polite to everyone, when all you want to do is lie down in a dark room with a cloth over your eyes and the curtains pulled and wish the world to go away -- if only for a little while. There were few times in a presidential candidate's days leading up to the election that they had time for themselves. Even my sleep was haunted with visions of the faces, the words, the merry-go-round that was American politics. I found my moments of solace in quiet prayers and the companionship of Jackie without whom, I freely admit, I would not have made it.

And in the end it worked, did it not?

After all the effort, the pain, the money, the travelling, the exhaustion, the doubts, for everyone has them, my parents had the pleasure of seeing their son elected President of the United States. I had to hope they were at last satisfied with their second son.

Reflections on the campaign battle
John Fitzgerald Kennedy looks back on the campaign trail

I look back on that pre-election time and wonder how I got through. The pain was intense; the strain on me was unbelievable; the strain on the marriage was almost too much to take. The family were supportive, but only to a certain degree. There were lingering problems between myself and my parents, the way they treated my disabled sister was a serious bone of contention which we never really did overcome, not in my eyes, anyway. From this distance of time I believe my relationship with the family was more love/hate than anything. Such support as I garnered from them was designed to push me into the White House to take my brother's place. I was not there for myself, not in their eyes, or so I believed. I am prepared to admit that I might be wrong on this, but all the indications were that I was being pushed; the second son had to become the first son and take on the role that the first son had ordained for him.

I am aware, through my extensive reading, that the 'second son' syndrome has haunted English history over many, many years. Now I was finding out for myself what it felt like, when the heir apparent dies for whatever reason and the second son has to step into my shoes. Sometimes it works, I thought, sometimes it doesn't. My determination was to make sure that this time, for the Kennedys, it worked.

I found it hard to sleep the night it was almost certain I had attained the highest office in the land. When I had the confirmation the presidency was mine, the feeling was almost unreal. Everything I had striven for, everything I had dreamed was finally there. The shock of actually making it to the top was great, the acceptance of having done it was a good deal more difficult than I realised. At first I was elated, then reality crashed in. Ahead of me lay the massive tasks of taking over the reins from a very popular president, one who was much loved, one who really had his finger on the pulse of the American people, in their eyes anyway. I had extensive overseas diplomacy to deal with, the problems at home to cope with; the critics who would say I was too young to take on the task, even though it was the will of the people. At times during the long day and even longer night, I felt I was inadequate to take on the job. By morning my resolve had returned, I knew that I would be a good president -- or die trying.

I made that comment and left the book for a while to think about it. I was busy talking from the depths of my heart, spilling all sorts of emotion onto these pages and only later wondering whether or not it was a good thing to do.

And then I thought, I am busy spilling all sorts of emotion onto these pages so that others might know how I felt at any time during my life. What I need to think about is how I feel now about spilling all this emotion. Despite the fact that some nights I did not come to work on the book, that some nights I came but was reluctant to speak, I had to admit it felt good. It was not often someone had the opportunity to release themselves from the burden of thoughts and memories, to allow them to go on with an easy mind. I had the opportunity, I was not about to let it go. Slowly but surely the draining away of memories, both good and bad, was having its effect in making me feel lighter, less anchored to life as I remembered it.

Reverting to my life story, I have to say that when I first entered the House there was no celebration at home, it was as if my acceptance, my election, was a foregone conclusion and the fact I could walk in and take my seat was a done deal. I did not see it that way; I considered it a major victory, not only politically but personally, fighting my unwilling body as well as the opponents who wanted to steal my votes. For me, entering the House was not a low key every day event, but I had to act as if it was. Have I said politicians have to be good actors, too? If I didn't, I should have.

I was a consummate actor. Throughout the campaign I had refused to admit to any health problems, sympathised with others who said they had problems, whilst knowing that I had far greater worries than they had. It was a deception, a calculated one, not wishing the American people to turn against me on those grounds. It was the ongoing battle of body against the spirit and I was determined to win. I would not allow my body to stop me being a good president, or my trying very hard to be a good president within my limitations. It meant concealing considerable pain from those who voted for me, it meant disguising the seriousness of some of the conditions from which I suffered; it meant ever offering a smiling face to the world no matter how I felt. It was not easy.

There were many celebrations within the family when I was elected president. If I thought at any time that some of those celebrations should have taken place when I first went into the House, I kept very quiet about it. It would not do to upset the family at such a critical moment, when all their ambitions had finally come home to do in the shape of one chronically disabled son who should never have been out on the campaign trail in the first place. But the thought remained, I could not shift it from my mind and although it did not spoil the celebrations, it certainly detracted from them in a small way. I realised that this was the first time, as far as I am concerned anyway, I had mentioned it. Black thoughts were mostly locked away in a place where they could do no harm. Yet another box marked 'bad memories.'

And at times I thought the inauguration would never come.

The days in between being elected and taking office are strange times. There is the need for discussion with the outgoing president, whether you wish to or not and there are busy days when you have to decide who is to be taken into government with you. I utilised the time to resolve the question of my Cabinet, to begin building fences with the Republicans and generally begin the groundwork for my presidency. I had a fine line to walk, not to surround myself with people younger than me who would be seen as yes-men and not wish to take on too many seasoned politicians so that it did not look as if I was incapable and needed to rely on their wisdom. I knew that when I began to dictate policy, to put into effect many of the things I wanted to put into effect, people would see that I was my own man. The task was to prepare them for that, not to give them false hope or to hand them any labels to attach in advance of my own policy making, for once a commentator pinned a label on someone, it was extremely difficult to remove. I did not wish to be categorised as the young aspiring Catholic who got be president by fluke, the margin of votes was narrow enough as it was, someone who then had to rely on older men to carry the presidency forward. The political life may well have boulders, potholes and other obstacles, it also had a quagmire and I was very cautious about stepping into it. Fortunately the young and attractive First Family had captured the imagination of a goodly proportion of Americans and it was to them that I would be speaking when I made my first speech. It had to be very carefully worded. And it would be.

Because I was the careful type of person, I had already commissioned someone to work out a transitional programme in the event of my winning the election. This made a big difference when I actually began to tackle the task of stocking the White House with the people I needed there, not the people others thought I needed there. The difference was quite extraordinary. There were those who said they had no experience, but I said I hadn't any experience either and we would learn together. By putting everyone on the same level as me, I created a different feeling in my administration. It was one committed to work and there was a good deal of that, but it was relatively free and easy. Top advisers had access to me as often as they needed it, so that it became more of a community, a circle of friends, then an administration. In many ways this was the secret of its success, at least in my eyes, because everyone was committed on levels, including their friendship with me.

It had been expected that the young enthusiastic president would bring an energy to the White House which would transform it, what they did not expect was that the president's wife would transform the White House.

I stand aside from my story for just a moment to say that my wife began the restoration of the White House against all advice, knowing that what she was doing was right. The decoration had to be altered, furniture had to be disposed of and new/old pieces found which fitted the time of the building. Once they were in place, Jackie ensured that they would not be removed in future, that they remained part of the White House and slowly but surely it became recognised that Jacqueline Kennedy and her designer friend were putting the White House back as it would have been - and it was magnificent. This added considerably to the status of the First Family, as opposition to her moves were overcome, as people began to realise that she was not just an ornament hanging onto the president's arm, but a person in her own right. It was partly this and partly Jacqueline's own personality which led to her being voted one of the most popular First Ladies. The obvious bond between the president and his wife made us an attractive couple and, I thought, if it had not been for my obsession, we would have been the perfect couple.

But more of that later. For the moment I wish to return to the time when I first entered the White House as I wish to relate my feelings concerning that.

There are many strands to this story, I thought, too much I need to talk about, but I'm afraid of losing the thread. I have paid homage to my wife's work in the White House and I also want to say she was a brilliant hostess regardless of who she had to entertain; she was a wonderful companion, mother, friend and wife. And yet, I could not stop pursuing other women. I knew that I was guilty at times of leading them on, of making more of my feelings for them than was actually there, allowing them to believe I would leave my wife for them. That would have been political suicide, but more than that, I would simply not have done it. Jacqueline was everything to me, regardless of who I was with, or how I felt about them. Had those women really known me, they would have realised that. But I knew well that women were – and are - often blinded to the truth by their own needs, which renders them completely incapable of seeing the truth in the person they were with. I understood this and made allowances for it, whilst knowing they really should have known better.

Diversions, diversions! It was time to go back to the arrival of John and Jacqueline Kennedy at the White House, at the start of what I believed would be a momentous presidency.

I mused that there are no words with which to describe the feeling of walking through the White House for the first time and hearing the words 'Mr President'. There are no words with which to describe the feeling of taking the oath of office and drawing onto yourself the mantle of responsibility of the most powerful position on the planet. As you stand with hand raised and recite the words that put you into that position, it is as if the world stands still just for you. I know I cannot not speak for other presidents, but that is how it felt to me. The taking the oath, the making of the oath, was a totally sacred moment in which I felt as if everyone was holding their breath and so made the earth stand still. The moment the words were uttered the noise, the shouts and the congratulations crashed in like a tidal wave to flatten the senses and almost overwhelm rational thought.

I remember the moment as being the most pivotal thing that had happened to me. That moment meant more than even being told I had won the election. For that was one thing, the actual taking the oath of office was another. And there are no words to describe my feelings.

Once the celebrations were done and the Inaugural Balls were over, the serious work began, taking care of business.

As the world knows only too well, that included women.

Halcyon Days

The first one hundred days of John Fitzgerald Kennedy's presidency.

If I had been aware of women before I became President, it became a hundred times worse once I got into the White House. I knew that power was an aphrodisiac, on both sides, but I hadn't appreciated how much of an aphrodisiac it was.

Throughout the campaign comments were made about my sexual activities: memorandums were passed around, allegations were made and at times it was almost as if these affairs would get in the way of my election. There were many who were unhappy about it, but as always my good nature, total commitment to the cause, natural ability to take on and conquer any 'enemy', including Richard Nixon, won the day for me. I often wonder if the fact that I seemed to be obviously heterosexual, had an overwhelming interest in women and seemed to have had many conquests during my life, actually added to my persona - as far as men were concerned. Secretly I was sure they admired someone who could bed so many women and get away with it, even if it came with an element of jealousy. I was quite sure that congressmen who criticised my sexual activity were no more than jealous. I admit I could be wrong, but I don't think so.

Once safely installed in the White House, with the campaign no more than a bad memory, I settled in to take up the reins of power and begin the job of attempting to put right the many things I saw were wrong with the American economy, the American overseas diplomacy and all the tasks that needed doing. For a time I was content to do this, but soon enough the restless sexual element came in, something I could not ignore. An addiction cannot be ignored, it can be put to the back of the mind for a short time, but it will always make its way forward again.

The simple fact was - I became the youngest president ever and the first Catholic one, too. My comparative youth was not something I thought about, as I felt perfectly competent and capable of handling the position, but I saw it broadcast in newspapers and on television and it got to me, put doubts in my head. My religion, too, was often mentioned. So, was I too young, did my religion matter? What would they have said had I succeeded in my bid four years earlier, then? I often asked myself and Jackie why it mattered so much how old or young I actually was or what my religion was. Neither of us had an answer. It was something I had to learn to live with and the only way to live with it was to get on with the job and prove that I was capable of doing it.

In addition to that determination, the mirror showed me a man maturing in a most pleasing way. I had been told I was charismatic and this, coupled with my looks, seemed to make me irresistible to women. I had always found it easy to make conquests, being in a position of such power made it even easier. The temptations were always there, women of all ages and positions in the White House seemed to be making an effort to dress and walk provocatively. A comment was made by one of the aides that the White House had become a much more interesting place with the arrival of the Kennedys, certainly more interesting than it had been in President Eisenhower's time. I wondered sometimes if they realised what a driving influence sex was, how much it affected people, consciously and subconsciously, with its ability to drive all rational thought out of a mind to leave the person only thinking with their body.

Which is exactly what I did. Within a tightly scheduled day I still found time for dalliances with those who were willing and there were many who were. I admit to many guilt trips, knowing that I should be faithful and loyal to Jackie and my family, but being totally incapable of committing myself to one woman. I knew well that Jackie knew of my sexual escapades, I knew too that it hurt her, but it was something we did not speak of. As always, I compartmentalised my life: the Presidency, Jackie and family, my sexual games. The boxes were not allowed to overlap and, with my rigidly disciplined mind, I was able to keep an eye on all that was going on in the White House and indulge my addiction at the same time.

The problem was, as always, I needed the adulation of women. Something that constantly escaped me was the answer to the question, why was not Jackie's adulation enough for me? She was everything I ever wanted in a wife, in a friend, in a partner, I should have been completely happy with her and never want to look at another woman. But I did.

My most infamous affair was with the film star Marilyn Monroe. Even as I thought about this book, even as the channel spoke with her editor about the book, Marilyn's name was constantly thrown into the ring. Each time I insisted – through my channel - that she was not the big secret I wanted to reveal, how could it be, when everyone knew of my association with her? no one took any notice. She was the one they had heard about so it had to be her. Well, dear reader, it isn't. But the revelation isn't coming yet. There is a way to go before then and a lot of ground to cover. Nothing in life is easy and life in the White House falls into that category, big time.

Women and politics. Was ever a man so plagued? I jest, of course. Politics was in my blood, women were in my heart. There was no way I could escape either of them, nor did I wish to.

The one thing I did learn during my 'waiting time,' as I thought of it, was that it was better to tackle the overseas diplomacy myself and let the others deal with the domestic problems in the interim. It looked better; actually a good deal of what goes on with the president in the White House is designed to look good rather than to do good but that is the way of political life. I knew before I took the Presidency that I wanted to build bridges with the Soviets, they being perceived by the American people as the biggest threat to our way of life. There was the pressing question of the two American flyers who had been shot down, they were released shortly after I took office. It had been negotiated, of course and, like everything else, was designed to make the President look good, as well as showing an attempted friendliness on the part of Mr Khrushchev. I was pleased, who would not be?

Here I go again, facts not feelings. I was a new president with new ideas, new enthusiasm, a new team and a burning desire to set right everything I thought and felt was wrong. Logically I know -- I knew then -- that no human being could do it all, not even if they lived for a couple of hundred years. There were and are just too many problems to be tackled. The present incumbent is finding out that this is so, just as I had to. Every decision you make has to be fought through the Senate, past the committees, past the disbelievers, the opponents, those who would choose any weapon to stab you in the back. Let me modify that; let me make it 'those who would choose any weapon to stab you in the chest' for they did it to your face and with a smile.

Now we're getting closer to the heart of the matter. Now we are peeling layers from the onion and finding that the bulb which remains within is capable of inducing tears. These are not manly but at times, in the sanctuary of my apartments, with Jackie's understanding, I did allow myself the solace of a few tears. I sometimes wondered why I had chosen a life that perpetuated my endless battle against my physical condition combined with the barbed wire pathway that was the Presidency. I hesitated before using that description, but then decided that it was the only way to demonstrate to those who have never walked it that the White House and all that it stands for is not paved with nice smooth flagstones but with something that feels remarkably like barbed wire. Some places you are able to walk without difficulty but then a spike is waiting to thrust itself into your foot. Over-dramatisation? Maybe. Then again, I do not think anyone can over-estimate the difficulties that a president has to cope with. Your high ideals, so carefully expressed throughout your campaign, applauded by all, are pounced upon as being from the very depths of the dark realm itself once you try to put them into practice. This has happened many times, not only in the USA, but in the UK and in Europe as well. A political party puts out its manifesto for everyone to read, it is their ambition to bring all these things into being but once elected, the reality becomes very different. First they find that some of it is not practical, they find that the opposition to the plans and aspirations are such that they cannot go ahead with it, or some lawyer finds a very good reason why it breaches this law or that. The voting public does not always understand this, nor do they understand that sometimes policies have to be brought in that are uncomfortable, stringent, or seemingly directly against their human rights, because everyone sees everything differently. So it is that any change, no matter how beneficial it might be, finds itself up against every opposition that it is possible for the people who oppose it to invent or discover.

There is heartbreak in this; many good policies which would benefit the people have fallen by the wayside because of overwhelming opposition. There comes a point when you cannot fight any longer, you have to stand back, admit defeat, then move on to the next thing you wish to push through. Then you find that when the mid-term elections come around, your popularity rating has gone through a radical change. Where you were once riding high, you are no longer Mister Nice Guy and are viewed with great suspicion. 'Who is this strange person?' they seem to ask. You long to reply; 'the person you voted in not so long ago.' You go and look at yourself in the mirror, you ask yourself are you not the same person who was applauded and lauded earlier as the saviour of the country? The answer of course is 'yes', it is just that they now perceive you in a different way. They have had a chance to see you, to understand that you are not superhuman, that you have to go with the majority because it is not a dictatorship; that all you have dreamt of cannot be done in one short term of office. Whilst the voters might understand this on a subliminal level, the conscious mind cries out 'but you promised' and indeed you did. You promised with all the conviction that you could generate, with all the passion that you could put into the speech and you had every intention of following through. What they fail to understand is you are one person standing against the tide of congressmen and senators and judges and protest groups and vigilantes... it cannot always be done. You can force through a policy with the narrowest of votes, but getting that policy onto the statute books is another matter entirely. It has to go past this committee and that and eventually it might go into law and at least one of your dreams might come true. Even as this happens, you are facing the next battle and the one after that and the one after that and you wonder why you ever wanted the job in the first place.

Which brings me back to the comments I made much earlier in this book, where I said it takes a very special person to become president. I say this without blowing my own trumpet, or asking for adulation, or even beginning to seek it, for the fact is that few people can walk on a barbed wire pathway and not decide it is too painful and think it would be a lot easier to step off to one side and walk on the smooth flagstones.

In between all this, barbed wire and all, there is another element – fear – that has to be contended with. Fear of poisoning, fear of 'accidents' that would take my life. With me sometimes on a walking cane, sometimes in a wheelchair, never entirely steady on my feet, how easy would it be for someone to 'create' an accident? How many 'ill health' presidents were actually poisoned and, through lack of forensic knowledge or simply a massive cover up, it was never known. I looked at every meal with suspicion, especially the big banquets where there would be a multitude of people to give alibis to any wannabe killer. Odd, isn't it, that I spent my presidency worrying about that but never gave a thought to a gunman. I would never have ridden in an open topped car if I had even slid a thought that way.

I had not written anything in my book for about two weeks; then I come back with some of the deepest and most intense thoughts I have had on the Presidency. I had rather surprised myself, not realising the depths of my feelings about this. But, you have come to this book wanting to read the raw JFK and here you have it. These are things I have never said to anyone at any time and here I am saying them to you, dear reader. It is my hope you appreciate it.

Thoughts on the administration
John Fitzgerald Kennedy in a pensive mood

That deviation from the narrative was longer than I anticipated, more in-depth than I anticipated, but it felt good and I realised I had wanted to say that since the book was started.

I'm not entirely sure where the idea came from to institute the Peace Corps. It was as if the concept arrived overnight full-blown. It was not there, then it was as if I had dreamed it and the dream was right. My idea of the Peace Corps worked in an odd way, one I had not anticipated, in that the Soviets looked on it with some suspicion, as did some other countries, which gave me an insight into their thoughts. But I was genuine in my desire to send the young people out there, ambassadors for the United States; in my eyes it worked.

One of the many problems I ran into was people looking for the hidden agenda behind everything I did. There were those who tried to dissect my reasons for the Peace Corps instead of accepting I really wished to put them out there in the world, to show the world that the US was capable of instigating peace, instead of war. I admit I grew impatient with those who tried to deconstruct everything I did, but had to accept that too was part of political life. When you are at the top, it is sometimes hard to remember that when you were lower down the pyramid you did exactly the same thing. It was a valuable point to remember from time to time.

I have never known people so quick to denigrate any idea that a president puts forward, always with the words 'this cannot be done'. I don't and didn't believe there was or is a single thing that couldn't be done, and it was this intense belief on the part of some Americans that put a man on the moon.

Now I want to make another small diversion. I am fully aware that there are a considerable number of people who do not believe it happened. They say that the reflections were wrong, that this was wrong, that was wrong and I say to them now - those men walked on the moon. The fact you have decided that this reflection and that reflection is not right, that this shadow is not right shows that you are not fully aware of the many strange lights that reflect onto the moon. You are not there. You are here. You are looking at this from the point of view of a person gravity bound on the third planet in from the sun. Neil Armstrong and Buzz Aldrin walked on the moon. They saw a different aspect of the sun, they saw a different horizon; they saw a different light from the stars. It changed them. I'm going to admit to you now that I was and still am overwhelmingly jealous that they were able to go and I was not. No way would I have been considered as an astronaut with my health record! Can you imagine it?

Right, back to the life story. My wish was that Mr Khrushchev would become friendly, if not actually a friend, to the United States. It would have been good to have dissipated the antagonism and fear shown toward the Soviets. Not that it would have made very much difference to the people of the USA, whatever we said and did they would continue to view the Soviet Bear as a threat, but it would have seemed a smaller threat and perhaps it would not loom so large in their minds. And I think to some degree that we did achieve at least a small breakthrough in what was generally known as the Cold War.

Did I like him? A difficult one to answer. I admired him as a leader, someone who controlled a vast country with untold millions of people, massive problems and massive wealth waiting to be tapped into and he seemed to have a grasp of European politics. As a man, though, he was difficult to understand, seeming to be behind a wall of his own building, as though he defied anyone to see or appreciate the real Nikita

Khruschev. We clashed over Cuba, but that is something for later in this narrative.

I did say to others I did not like him. I guess in part that has to be true, but I also have to say that no one ever gives a totally honest opinion of anyone at any time. I truly was unhappy with someone I could not begin to know.

I never did discover what he thought of me. In common with most people, I tended to think that I was easy to read, but I do know that was not right. We all have many layers, some more than others, but more than that, we do tend to put on a face that fits each person that we are speaking with. As in, I was a completely different person when with my wife and family than I was sitting behind the desk in the Oval Office. Then I was President, before that I was husband and father. Do we not all do this? Do we not all slot into the various roles which we have allocated for ourselves in our lives? Are we not at any given time a son, a brother, a cousin, a father, a grandfather (for those who live that long) a nephew, a friend... it goes on and you know well the roles you are called upon to play. In politics this role-playing can be multiplied by a factor of ten at times. You have to stop and tell yourself who you really are. If you think some presidents have along the way lost their grasp on politics, their politics, this is the reason why. They have lost track of who they really are. It is very easy for the public - I use the term loosely and without condemnation - to only see the public face of the president. The smiling, confident, assured person who appears on their television sets is an image they hold and believe in. Contrarily, this is what the White House staff is aiming for. It does make it very difficult for the public to then understand that the president is in fact a human being. As such, he will make mistakes, he will fall prey to the vagaries of the human mind, as in being distracted by ill-health, by lust, by love and I will be honest here and say by the sheer intoxicating feeling that power brings. There are times when that power swamps and sometimes obliterates the common sense that the human being who has been appointed as president once had.

I have to go back to the same point that I made before - did I in fact make it? - Having written so much, and thought so much, I am in danger of losing track of my own narrative! Whichever way it is, let me say it now. We are human beings with all the frailties that being human brings; we who are appointed to the highest office in the Western world. Yes, here I bow to the might, the strength, the political magnitude of the leader of the Soviet Union, whoever they are. There had been a few since Mr. Khruschev joined me on this side of life.

Because we are human beings, we err, just as you do. Our errors tend to be a good deal bigger, but they are usually the result of an imbalance of advice from two conflicting sources - the right and the left of whatever political stance the President holds. Pressures are put on him that are extremely difficult to handle, he is asked to do the impossible in many ways, basically to please everyone. As president you have to listen to both sides, you have no choice. If you did not he would upset the one or the other and that would not do. It was also good to listen to both sides and make up your mind, having weighed both arguments. But in the end it comes down to your own individual judgement, how and where and when the decision is made is a decision in itself. Make it too soon and you look as though you have rushed it. Take too long in deciding and you look as though you are indecisive. There are times when the barbed wire pathway can appear to be nothing but spikes.

I would say without fear of contradiction that everything I have said in this particular section of my story applies to every single leader in every single country around the world where there is a democracy. Only dictators live without the constant pressures of having to listen to both sides, then make a decision on what they have heard and to try and make that decision in such a way that it does not look as if you are rushed or you are indecisive. Nothing is as simple as it seems.

I make no secret of the fact when I got into office I wanted a test ban treaty. It was the sort of nightmare scenario that no American wanted to live with. That included me. I had in mind also it would help me to build bridges with the Soviets if we went down that route and anything that would help me to do that, I was prepared to do. In everyone's life there has to be a direction, a directive, an ambition: mine was to build bridges so that the USA would feel a safer place to live. How much of that was psychological and how much of that was actual is anyone's guess, but what is in the mind is often more potent than that which is written on paper. I knew my fellow Americans feared and hated the Soviets, feared the thought of nuclear attack and so I decided to make it one of the points of my presidency. Fortunately my staff was with me on this: I met with no disagreements whatsoever when the subject was discussed. What I had to do was to work out how to approach the subject with the Russian leader and get it into practice. Simple enough, is it not?

It is truly ironic that I have concluded the last two paragraphs with the word 'simple' somewhere. I said first that nothing is as simple as it seems and then I said simple enough, is it not?

In politics nothing is as simple as it seems, for there are too many voices to be heard, too many opinions to be taken into consideration, too many voters whose loyalty needs to be maintained if you are to continue with your policies in the way you want. If you lose the loyalty of the people, they will badger their congressman into putting their point of view across which may well conflict with your own. I think that should read it will conflict with your own. That issue is never in doubt.

Carrying this forward into negotiations with the Soviets, you will understand that although the concept was simple, America and the Soviet Union should discuss a treaty on nuclear weapons, the actuality was something else. It was fraught with difficulties because the Soviets appeared to feel more vulnerable than anyone had realised and so they were more anxious for nuclear defence than we had anticipated. It was just another conundrum which had to be resolved if there was to be peace in the world.

I had to walk a fine line between committing ourselves to a prohibitively expensive programme of nuclear defence and not antagonise the rest of the world. Where to draw the line? When do you say 'we have more weapons than you and can kill more people than you and so you would be foolish to start a war with us' and when do you say 'we are even now and we would wipe each other out and how stupid would that be?' All of this had to be said without being said, if you understand my meaning. All this had to be expressed diplomatically through translators, which made it even more difficult, with both of us nodding and smiling and acting as if we knew exactly what the other one was doing. In the end, of course, we both drew back from the brink because we had to. It would have been foolish to do otherwise. But I did have an ongoing battle with the military which seemed to think they had the entire nuclear war in their hands and could do just as they wished provided I authorised the first launch. I had to take this presumption from them without damaging those huge military egos. I think I can honestly say it was the most difficult task of my entire time in the White House. Having had experience of military hierarchy, I knew well it would not be easy.

One of my other difficulties was attempting to keep the Soviets out of Africa. Again, a diplomatic tightrope if you like, with LBJ flaunting around with his ballpoints, etc. I smiled a good deal as I watched him do this, being a typical Texan, because as a PR exercise it had everything I wanted, Texan extravagance and loads of attention. Africa was really too big a continent for me to tackle in any real form and perhaps I should have left well alone, but at the time it seemed like a good idea. Come to think of it, so was Laos. Both these major incidents are well documented, I'm not really sure I can add anything to them. I am not even sure that you would want me to; because I am trying to walk a diplomatic tightrope here too, in that I want to give you my feelings at the time but do not wish to get heavily into politics and bore you to death. It is a moot point which I have discussed with my channel, which part of my life is most important: women or politics? Having given the matter some considerable contemplation, I have decided there is nothing to choose between them. In many ways I have to say my presidency, my political ambitions, my desires to make life better for my fellow Americans, did take precedence over just about everything else. Family life was extremely important to me and still is. The women were my outlet, my escape from the pressures of the presidency, of being high profile, of being virtually crippled by my back condition, of trying to be the perfect husband and father. In a normal life it is extremely difficult to be a perfect husband and father, if you add the pressures that living in the White House brings then any relationship comes under the most immense strain. It needs an outlet. As I have already explained in detail which is sure to bring the comment 'too much information', it was a tremendous relief for me, one that was addictive. In your world today you have clinics for those who are supposed to have sex obsession. Fortunately for me there was no such thing.

149

Feelings. Not politics. Very difficult for me. I grew up with a political background, listening to discussions, most of which I did not understand at the time. Children absorb emotions, outlooks, bias, all manner of things from their parents and so all of us absorbed politics. That is why Joe, Bobby, Teddy and I all went into politics as a career. The fact that for Joe there was no future past his bomber pilot days is a tragedy, for he had an astute and ultra-logical mind which would have stood him in very good stead in the political arena. That task fell to me as the second son, closely followed by Bobby and Teddy. But Bobby's life was cut short as mine was and Teddy's career was damaged by the Chappaquiddick accident. Having said that, he went on to be a most revered Senator, which pleased me very much, watching from this side of life. No matter what supposed skeletons the media raked up about his life and his activities, he became a sort of senior statesman and carried the Kennedy name proudly for a good many years. I am grateful to him for this; in many ways he took on the role I expected of my son who did not live to fulfil his potential. There are people who say the Kennedys are cursed and there is much to be said for this theory, because it does seem as if we had more than our share of bad luck as far as death is concerned. But it has to be remembered that we are a large family and in any large family there will be tragedies. That is even more likely when members of the family are extremely high profile, as we were.

There are good things about being a president; you can get your own way on a good many things, you have the very best of food and medical attention and other things which make life pleasant, you get to travel in luxury and everywhere you go people seem pleased to see you. Your name and face, every word you speak in public, the clothes you wear, are broadcast across the nation's newspapers all the time. If you are an egoist you have no difficulty with this. No person who is a shy, retiring wallflower would ever become president, because of the intense public scrutiny to which you are subjected the moment you become involved in politics in the first place. This is leaving aside the campaigning, when everyone seems determined to bring you down, no matter how good your policies are or how sincere you are in your desire to help your fellow Americans. It is difficult to learn to live with. I know Jackie found it extremely difficult but she learned, as we all do, to adopt the smiling poker face which tells everyone absolutely nothing.

And then there was Cuba. In many ways this was a more difficult conundrum than the Soviet one, surprising when you consider the disparity in size of the two countries.

A (long) time of reflection
John Fitzgerald Kennedy takes time out to work and to think

That was where we stopped in 2015. The word 'Cuba' halted me for a while and I needed time to think. To remember. Then other things got in the way, family guidance needed from this side of life, my channel's busy life including a major bereavement and yes, I admit it, I am making excuses. Not for her, she cannot work if I am not here dictating; the delay has been down to me.

So, Cuba. I can't escape it this time, but – I do have my brother Bobby here to help me phrase this properly. My memory is of intensive, ongoing held-breath negotiations. You could call them that but really it was a question of two leaders with their heels firmly dug in and their standing and honour with their people at stake. I could not be seen to be weak but I could not be seen to be the one who obliterated the known world. Apart from any other consideration, in the dark hours when sleep walked the grounds of the White House and so did not venture near my bedroom, I did not want to be locked in an underground bunker for – how long? With people I would quickly learn to dislike and eventually to hate? I also asked myself, what was the point of running to underground bunkers for survival if the rest of the world had vanished in radioactive dust? What was the point of living? Who would benefit from my being alive?
    If you can imagine this kind of nonsensical dialogue going on in my head, then you will get a tiny inkling of the messed up thought processes I was going through at the time. I have to say the Excomm tapes are dull listening for the most part, but then they become more interesting as the discussions get wilder. That's a mirror image of my night time deliberations. I am surprised the film and photos of me at that time show a reasonable

looking person. I felt haggard, shattered; ill of course, that goes without saying; the stress levels were so high I thought I'd end up in hospital again. How would that go down with the people of the USA? I take them into a missile crisis with their most hated enemy and then end up in hospital and let others sort it out... my standing would have been reduced to about zero by the time I got out. So I kept quiet about that and spent all my time being the fearless, unbeatable President they (I hope) thought I was. Inside I was a mess of indecision, determination, worry, pain and downright fear. If the plans went wrong, I would be the last President the USA ever had.

Bobby's laughing. There's a lot here he's never known, I've never told him, not wanted to allow him to think less of me than he does. *How stupid of you*, he just said, *you're a Kennedy; you can do no wrong.*

He's finding that line really amusing, and it takes a lot to amuse the straight-laced lawyer that is my brother. Come to think of it, yes, it is an amusing line, never knew I had it in me to write nonsense like that. I should have let myself go a few times at cocktail and diplomatic parties, not fought for the right words at the right time. It might have broken the ice a bit more with those who mattered in the world political arena. Too late, Jack, too late... as I have been with a lot of my thoughts. Like, too late to swap to a closed in armoured car to travel through Dallas. Right?

The diplomatic game, I almost wrote The Game of Diplomacy but that doesn't fit as well, is one that millions are playing around the world at any moment. The difference is; you now live in a totally intrusive technological age and risk being exposed at any moment. So the diplomatic game has become a dangerous one, you can't tell any more if you're being filmed or recorded. Yes, I arranged to record the ExComm meetings, they were critical to the survival of the USA and the world. I might have needed to release extracts if anything had gone wrong – the complete tapes are in print if you really want to wade through them – but this is different, this is dirt digging, this is spite, this is vindictive behaviour through all the forms of social media. It is best left alone. From the highest to the lowest, it is dangerous. Lives can be shattered by silly casual comments which once upon a distant time would not have been allowed to escape into the world and the person be vilified for having said them.

Enough. I am stating the obvious, but few of you seem capable of staying away from the various outlets where you can vent your anger, your thoughts, your innermost secrets, if you so desire. The channel does not touch them, it's one of the reasons we entrust her with our words.

I was a physical wreck after that fortnight of nerves and worries, of finding the right diplomacy, of working out how to evade confrontation without losing face. Oh the ever present need of not wanting to lose face! But to do so would be to damage any standing I had in the world, and by 'I' you can take it as meaning my party, staff, advisors and family – not necessarily in that order, either.

In the dark hours I talked with, or spoke to, my channel, knowing she would remember it come morning - and she did. My words were: 'what is it you want from me?'

These words will cut to the heart of every person who stands for public service. Every living being wants something different from the politician before them. Every single one. They may think they have the same desires and aspirations as the next-door neighbour but that isn't true. Every single one has something different they need, they desire, they demand of their public servant. When that 'something' is not delivered, the outrage is extreme. If you think about it, you will realise it is the way of the political world. Politicians, wannabe politicians especially, make promises they cannot fulfil and would not be able to fulfil if they were in office for the next hundred years or so. There is not enough money, not enough space, not enough time to implement every single thing the politician promises – even though he tries and tries very hard.

The first thing that happens when a new President is elected is the Senate ranges itself against him – or her, should that happen – even though there is on surface an air of 'we're all good friends here, let's work together for the betterment of the people of the USA.' It's false. It's false because they know the outline of the President's aims and ambitions for his first term of office and it doesn't always match their pet aims and ambitions. Why should it? We are individuals with our own ideas of what the country needs, to the point when we are prepared to throw goodness knows how much money into the electioneering to put ourselves in a position of leadership to promote and further our own aims and ambitions, not each individual senator. It's very much like one big happy family, especially for the party whose nominee has achieved the high office, being content to celebrate until the gifts are opened and then the disappointment sets in. So the first thing they do is gang up on the new president and make every effort to block every reform he wants to bring in, on the grounds it doesn't suit their voters. With so many states and so many people of so many diverse and contradictory cultures, how could one man produce a manifesto the country can follow which would suit every single person in that country?

The art of negotiation is an acquired talent, earned after countless battles with hecklers, political commentators, journalists who think they know more than the person they're questioning and the press generally. It's learning to walk the cobweb bridge, the one separating the newly elected from the old school packing into the House with determination to 'spike the new President's guns' written all over them.

It's not much fun, the word 'gladiator' comes to mind and sometimes that's the point when you stop and ask yourself, what the hell am I doing here?

The answer depends on the person. My first thought was, I can't do this; my second was, hell, I can!

I'd give a lot to know what the thoughts of my predecessors were on this subject. We can't escape the burdens of presidential office. No matter how laid back we want to appear, inside it's a turmoil of exhaustive and exhausting worries and endless pressures. I think the pressures were the worst part of the whole job. That fortnight of waiting to see if I would be the one responsible for ending the world... created a pressure that's impossible to describe. I don't know even now how I lived through it.

My days and most of my nights were taken up with the box containing all my political decisions, needs, worries, successes and dreams, being thrown around in my mind, tumbling over itself, all these disparate issues falling foul of each other, as the needs gave way to the worries, as in 'I can't get/do/have/achieve...' whatever that particular issue needed. Or, Jackie needs me but I have to go talk to this group and that group, so need to prepare a speech before I go and what about the children, wouldn't they like to see their father occasionally? And...

And... would any of us Presidents have walked out on the job unless we were driven to it? Did any of us abdicate because we couldn't stand it any longer? Hell, no. Most of us fought for re-election when our first term was up, we spent the first term campaigning to ensure we got the second one at least. And then, the life of leisure awaited us. Some of us. Poor Ronald never got a life of leisure; the cruel illness took him from the world.

I feel desperately sorry for First Ladies, it's the toughest job on earth, coping with the demands of an entire nation prepared to savage you for the wrong word, the wrong colour dress, the wrong dress, even for being married to the President – it felt that way sometimes and Jackie has since confirmed it's how it felt to her. Somehow the population manage to overlook the fact that most people are married when they achieve high office, the First Ladies don't marry a President. They don't even marry a wannabe at times. Jackie did but not all First Ladies have that ambition.

It's no walk in the Rose Garden at the White House, whether you're President or First Lady. That's why, in a lot of ways, I wasn't that sorry it all ended. We'll get there; I needed to say all this first and at least I did some work tonight. I've been MIA for a few days, Bobby and I had things to talk through before I committed them to paper.

Sorry about that…

Dallas – and afterlife

John Fitzgerald Kennedy reaches the end of his mortal life

And so… Dallas.

The problem I have is that the very name of the place can still send ice cold chills down my spiritual spine. It would seem that, despite the passing of time, your time, the impact of that particular bullet has not gone away. I can and do relive it often and am aware of the many books and theories on the assassin, alone or with help and his/their reasons why I should be such a nuisance to the world someone needed me taken out of it.

If I could for a moment revert to the time when someone fired a gun at Ronald Reagan, I want to ask, did he have the same questions afterwards? Why me, why then, what had I done that someone wanted me dead?

One of the things Bobby and I talked through was our reaction to our deaths. If you think that's an odd thing, well, let me throw this thought in your direction – you're not there yet but when you are, if you died in a car crash, falling down stairs, ending up in the sea or a lake, getting trapped in a fire – whatever it is, you'll find yourself thinking about it on and off, wondering if you could have avoided it. Answer – no. Like all of us, you chose the life before you came, and you chose the way you would leave it. I can't remember agreeing to an assassination, nor can Bobby, come to that but we must have done, as that was how it happened.

And yes, I know, I'm stalking around the topic rather than confronting it.

So, at last, let me confront it.

Dallas. I was looking forward to the visit, I had speeches written and partially memorised; I knew who I was going to meet and planned everything to fit them.

Jackie had new outfits to stun the fashion world and her fans out there in the countryside and town. We talked with excitement of visiting Dallas. It was important to us to generate excitement about our visits; otherwise they would all have been the same round: faces, food, crowds, pack up, move on.

Sunshine. Lots of open topped cars. Lots of people with cameras or waving madly and smiling and I did a lot of smiling right back at them, wondering how many would vote for me next time, if I got the nomination, if I got the backing, if, if, if… sometimes idle thoughts are a waste of time, aren't they? But see me in the limousine, in the sunshine, my beloved wife by my side, see me smiling and acknowledging the crowds and then see me fall sideways towards my beloved wife. That was the moment of my transition from life to no-life.

If I registered the sound of the gun, I don't recall it, but then there was so much noise at my level, car engines, motorcycle engines, roars of the crowd, tyres on the road, (we'll let the English spelling stand, it actually makes more sense than tires, which is how the whole campaign was affecting me anyway. To me it was like being punched violently in the head and neck. So violently I couldn't sit up and couldn't stop the blackness rushing in, taking over, shutting out the sunshine and the screams. Someone told me there were screams. Surely there were, presidents don't get shot in a state of total silence and isolation.

Then I was there, distanced, quite a distance as far as I could work out, not quite one of the crowd, not quite hanging round heaven's door waiting to go in. Somewhere in between. I could see my body, surprisingly solid looking, considering I was still conscious of it and wondering why I wasn't getting up and looking around. You see how tangled the thoughts were? My heart and mind were screaming for Jackie, wanting her to hold me and tell me everything was all right, just a prank, just a fire cracker going off, that's all, but the look on her face, blank, emotionless, like a robot going through the motions as the car took off for the hospital at speed, told me what I thought had happened, had really happened. Assassinated. Done. No more White House, no more campaigning, no more battles with senators, no more anything.

It was about then the shock of it hit me and although I followed the cavalcade and saw the body being taken into the hospital, saw the shocked looks, saw the tears, all I could feel was the loss, the tremendous loss of the years ahead with my wife and children, with my brothers and other family members. The loss of another term of office – I was that sure I would get in – the loss of the projects I wanted to push through, so many things hitting me like a fusillade of bullets. That was a joke, if you consider it, a bullet took me from life and there I was with thoughts hitting me like bullets. Oh, good one, Jack.

I was alone, or so I believed, not sure how I was walking but remembering the sensation of walking, wanting to know what was going on, wanting to be there at the inauguration of Lyndon Johnson, wanting to wallow in bitterness and sorrow as he took my place at the head of our country. It didn't happen. Not the inauguration, the law insisted we had a President and so he was duly elected to the high office. It didn't happen for me to see. Instead I turned around to begin walking and was confronted by my brother Joe, arms wide open, huge smile, saying the words I hadn't realised I'd been longing to hear for more years than I cared to remember, 'well done, Jack!'

Last thoughts

John Fitzgerald Kennedy ends his thoughts on his truncated life

It was a lot of years ago, in your time, that is. I have not been forgotten, that's obvious and very comforting. It's always a compliment when people say 'I remember where I was when I heard the news.' Not many events generate that kind of memory trigger.

For me, I had to stand back and watch my children grow up, my wife find a new husband, Lyndon Johnson go his own way with the policies we had in place. I had to watch the returning Vietnam Vets and mourn over the losses – far too many.

I had to watch the Presidents the American people voted in and kept my thoughts to myself on the abilities and character of all of them. I especially do that right now.

I spend a lot of time helping family members, even if they don't know I'm there and working for them and with them. They just know sometimes the pathway is smoothed out and they move on without giving it a thought. It's fine, I'm grateful I can do something.

Thanks for buying this, thanks for reading this. It's taken too long to get into print, I know that but there were consultations and heart searches and all sorts – you know how it goes.

Right now my channel is waiting for the final words to conclude this book, another for her collection of channelled works. She's waiting for me to put a label on one of my mental boxes, one I haven't mentioned – deliberately – throughout this book. It's the one dark secret I retained up to now.

The box is labelled
MEN.

Thanks go to:

John Fitzgerald Kennedy for entrusting me with his story and in consequence of that, his future happiness and progression as a spirit;

Jacqueline Bouvier Kennedy for her help and input, agreeing with her the male ego is so supreme the females in this world need to moderate it and work around it so the truth is revealed...;

Robert Francis Kennedy for being there for his brother and me;

Lynne Mulrooney for the amazing amount of help;

Mary Holliday, devoted friend;

Ann-Jacqueline Davies, devoted friend;

Terry Wakelin because he was and is Terry Wakelin, my rock and my anchor as always, no matter on which side of life he happens to be;

My constant companions for their support, love, guidance, laughter and for always being there.

Special mention must be made of my publisher, Stuart Holland, who believes in the books, in the subjects and in me. Without his input and ongoing help, this book would not have been written. Jack Kennedy and I give you our sincere and grateful thanks.